A CAN
and

'We were on our way to the pub when we found it; that was when my friend did the drawing, me, Alan and an art student called Althea. I remember her because she and Alan got very friendly that night and agreed to meet again the following evening.

'"Where?" said Althea.

'"Oh, at the settee," said Alan. That was what started it, really. Because, naturally, the following evening the settee had gone elsewhere, but Alan didn't know where Althea lived and she didn't know where Alan lived, so they had to find it. We finally located it down a side street by the main Post Office, and Althea was there before us. After that it became a routine; "See you at the settee."'

ALSO BY JAN MARK

Enough is Too Much Already

A CAN OF WORMS
and other stories

JAN MARK

A Red Fox Book

Published by Random Century Children's Books
20 Vauxhall Bridge Road, London SW1V 2SA

A division of the Random Century Group

London Melbourne Sydney Auckland
Johannesburg and agencies throughout
the world

First published by The Bodley Head Children's Books 1990

Red Fox edition 1992

Printed and bound in Great Britain by
Cox & Wyman Ltd, Reading, Berkshire

ISBN 0 09 987160 2

For Imogen Woodings

Contents

I

The Travelling Settee

When I saw the results that the others were getting I knew that a special effort was called for. The assignment was to produce, over the summer holiday, an in-depth study of your favourite author, which was amended, just before the end of term, to 'an author whose work you admire', as it turned out pretty quickly that half the class had the same favourite author who was shortly going to receive eleven identical questionnaires. We had to check with Mrs Montgomery to make sure that we all came up with somebody different which was tough on the ones who'd only read one book ever in their entire lives.

It wasn't tough on me. I've always read a lot. I chose an admired author and typed out a grovelly letter and a list of questions, and sent it off to her publisher with a polite note asking them to forward it, but perhaps it was them I should have grovelled to, because they didn't. What I got back was a sort of publicity hand-out with a list of answers to questions I hadn't asked and I could tell from those that I would never have got answers to the questions I *had* asked, like, 'Do you ever feel dissatisfied with a book after it's published?' and 'Could you name any other authors you particularly admire?' This lady obviously never feels dissatisfied with anything she's done, and as for admiring anyone else, well, I looked at the photograph on the back of her last novel and I could just hear her saying, 'Dahling, what an extraordinary suggestion!' I decided to read that one again and then do a hatchet job on her (*Grossly overrated hack, A S Lampson . . .*) but then about the second week of the holidays some of us began comparing notes, and I had to think again.

I'd assumed that we'd all be having the same problem, but no. I'd drawn the short straw. All the other authors had sent nice letters back. Some said they were a bit busy and hoped that this would be what was wanted; one had written by hand and it took three of us most of the morning to decipher it, and a couple sent information sheets like the Lampson job, but they'd written extra things on to answer particular questions. And there was me with my miserable hand-out. It was a reasonable mistake—choosing her, I mean—because the characters in her books are all intuitive and sympathetic and spend hours sitting around in their stripped pine kitchens listening to each other's troubles, which is just as well, as there'd be no book if they didn't. No one ever *does* anything. Next time I read one of hers, if I ever do, I shall know it is all a sham. If *she* ever sits around listening to people's troubles it is probably because she is memorizing them all to use in her next novel. Meanwhile I had only four weeks left to start all over again with my in-depth study and I had my reputation to consider. I always do well in English. I've always been teased for spending so much time reading. I'd been sure of getting a Grade A in GCSE and now it looked as if I was going to hand in a real bummer while Mrs Montgomery looked at me more in sorrow than in anger, saying, 'Oh, Bridget, I'd have thought you would have done better than this,' and everybody else got the Grade As.

It was due to be handed in on the first day of term, too, and I knew that if it wasn't I was going to get behind with everything else, just trying to catch up. I went to sit on my bed and stare at the books on my shelves. Which lucky novelist was going to hear my letter hitting the mat? (*Congratulations, Mr Golding. You have been selected to star in my forthcoming assignment.*)

I keep my favourite books under the window in a special bookcase with other treasures. Mum calls it my shrine. I went through the writers' names; seven had been chosen by other people in the class, one of them had been struck off after I saw him interviewed on television and he said things so racist and sexist and generally nasty that I began to wonder why he bothers with books. I'm sure he'd be happier writing for A Certain Newspaper. The other eighteen were dead. Sensible fellows; no one was writing to them asking why they had become authors. Were you good at English at school, Miss Brontë?

Then I noticed three books at the end of the shelf that had been there so long that I didn't even see them any more, the first books that I'd ever bought for myself, years ago. I loved them. I read them over and over again, in fact, the reason I bought them was that I kept taking them out of the library and getting withdrawal symptoms if someone else had got there first, till my mother said, 'For heaven's sake, *have* the things,' rather as if she was giving me the money to go out and get stoned, so I did, and then I had a great binge, reading straight through, one–two–three, several times in a row. After that I got diverted to someone else and didn't open them again for—well, until that moment. But they were the beginning of my collection.

You know how it is when you're in love; everybody seems slightly out of focus except the person you're in love with. I think I was in love with those books; nothing else I read then seemed to mean very much; not that the stories were nonsense, but the words themselves had no—no edge. But I never felt I was in love with the author, I never thought about him at all, and yet he lives in our town, only about a mile away. I didn't know that then, and when I found out I was past caring because I'd moved on to other books; but as I sat there, looking at that row of spines, I suddenly thought, Why not? Why not write about *him*?

I looked him up in the phone book to see if he was still there, and he was; James Rudd, 56 Marlowe Road, but in a way I couldn't be sure that it was still him. He wrote those three books years ago, before I was born; they were in paperback when I got them; and then he stopped.

I knew this because I'd checked on him in the library after I'd decided to get in touch, and he'd only written one other book, about eighteenth-century architects, which was what made me think I might be on to something different. One of the questions we had all asked our author was: Why did you begin writing? What I wanted to ask James Rudd was: Why did you stop? and then I had my best idea of all. I wrote to him, but I didn't include a questionnaire. I put:

Dear James Rudd,

I have always admired your books. In fact I have read them so many times that I almost know them by heart. As I am doing an assignment on my favourite author for GCSE, would you please allow me to come and interview you? As you can see I

don't live very far away, so I could call at any time convenient to you.
Yours sincerely,
Bridget Galvin

'Send him a stamped addressed envelope, that'll soften him up,' my mother advised.

After I'd posted it I began to wonder what I'd let myself in for. As I'd discovered from the Loathesome Lampson, authors are not necessarily what they seem from their books and as I said, I never thought much about what James Rudd might be like, while I was reading him, but I suppose I'd always had at the back of my mind the idea that the person who'd written those books must be kind, and rather serious and thoughtful; but a lot could have happened in seventeen years. He might have gone mad, for instance, or become poverty-stricken and vicious; a wife-beater; a drunk. Maybe I wouldn't be safe with him and would come screaming out of the house with my dress torn.

Then I realized that I ought to read the books again, because if he'd changed, so had I, and that meant the books would have changed, too. And the awful, awkward thing was, I didn't want to read them again in case I was disappointed. I read almost anything in those days. A good book was a book I enjoyed reading; I didn't care if it was well written or not because I couldn't tell. In the four days between posting my letter and getting his reply, I tried to nerve myself to read at least one of them again, but I kept putting it off.

'I ought to do the weeding first,'—that shows how distracted I was—or, 'Perhaps he won't even answer I'll get on with my Geography assignment instead,' but in the end, just in time, I got out of bed one morning and grabbed a book, it was the last one, without giving myself a chance to debate about it. I opened it at random, it opened itself, really, at a page I'd pressed flat and split the spine. And I read,

He stared, turned the bicycle and went back, and saw that it had not been an illusion. At the end of the cul-de-sac stood a street lamp, the old-fashioned kind that had once been lit by gas, and beyond it was the mouth of an alley. He dismounted: it was never wise to approach too quickly, and wheeled the bicycle down the middle of the deserted street, keeping his eyes fixed on the shadowy opening, and as he drew near he saw that it was a gas light: and he knew that he was right: he was about to find the garden again.

Relief; he used too many ands in my opinion, but it wasn't illiterate rot. I could go back safely and read the rest, but before I could even turn to the first page Mum called up from the hall, 'Letter for you! It looks as if the waters have returned your bread.'

We met on the stairs and she was holding out an envelope with my writing on it. Rudd had written.

Actually, he had typed, on a proper typewriter, not a word processor.

Dear Miss Galvin,

Thank you for your flattering letter. I am at home this weekend so perhaps you would care to call on Sunday afternoon? I have been living with GCSE assignments for two years, so understand that time may be of the essence.

Yours sincerely,

and then there was a tatty signature that could have said anything.

'Oh,' I said, still on the stairs with Mum. 'Do you think that means everyone's doing assignments on him?'

'No,' she said, 'I think it means he's got kids your age who usually leave school work to the last minute.' She gave me a heavy look.

I sent him a postcard saying yes, thank you, and settled down to read the books again, just like I had when I was a kid, holed up in the bedroom with food at hand, charging right through, one–two–three, without even stopping between books. And I was right. One of us had changed, me or the books.

It was one of those days that makes you realize how near to autumn August is. It was warm, sunny, but there was a sharpness about it that you don't notice in July. In July you can still smell things growing, especially after rain, but in August you know the end's coming. The sunlight's paler. Some of the leaves have turned; the air tastes brown, not green. But I like autumn and that Sunday I walked across town to Marlowe Road, down the path beside the park and across the allotments, where there were bonfires burning, making the light hazy. That says 'Autumn' to me, too.

I could see the end of Marlowe Road all the way across the allotments. There was a little alley leading out of them with a plank bridge over a ditch, that ran alongside the back garden of the end house. As I went down it I noticed that there was an old-fashioned street lamp at the end, but not so old-fashioned it would have run on gas. Still, it made me think of the books.

Of course, I had been thinking about the books all the way, but mainly I had been rehearsing what I was going to say, and trying *not* to imagine what James Rudd would turn out to be like, because I couldn't even guess, any more. I knew now that I had loved those books because I had felt at home in them, safe, certain. What I had never noticed when I was ten, eleven, twelve, was how terribly sad they were. I don't mean they were gloomy, they weren't, they were quite funny a lot of the time which is probably why I read them in the first place, but this time, when I came to the end of the last one, I felt really upset, as if I had lost something, almost tearful. It could have been partly because my period was due, but there was definitely something in those books that hadn't been there three years ago, that I hadn't been able to see, three years ago. I knew then, as I passed the lamppost, that I was going to meet a dreadfully unhappy man.

All the way across the allotments I'd been wondering if I was looking at the backs of the even numbers and, if so, which one was 56, but now I saw that 56 was the third house on the other side, the left-hand one of a pair of semi-detached villas, the kind that seem to squat there, bottom heavy, immovable, like Sumo wrestlers. The word *slab* comes to mind when I see houses like that. It was a nice-looking place, though, with a white front door. All the windows were open. Upstairs someone was playing a clarinet.

Often when I turn up for an appointment I arrive too early out of nervousness, and walk up and down outside till it's time to ring the bell. But all those open windows! I was probably being watched, and I hadn't been given an official time to call, so I walked straight up to the front door and knocked, because the bell was your average belly-button, but the knocker was iron, and old, a woman's face with a most evil smile. I liked her and gave her a few good thumps. Immediately the clarinet stopped and a door banged and voices started yelling, 'Dad! *Dad! DAD!*' Mum had been right about the children.

I looked at the front garden, which was full of little clipped bushes, and pretended not to hear the racket inside, because clearly it had not occurred to them that I would hear. I began to get dingy visions of the interior; a pram in the hall, a smell of cats, worn lino, washing on a clothes-horse in front of the fire and—Good God! Rudd himself in a tin bath on the hearth rug, while his wife scrubbed his back. Straight off the telly; D. H. Lawrence, I expect.

Then a face looked out of a bay window overhead and shouted, 'He's in the garden. Can you go round the side?'

I had just time to see that it was a girl about my age, right again, Mum, before it withdrew and the clarinet started up. I went back off the steps and down along the side of the house, which was the usual network of drainpipes and tiny windows, through a high wooden gate and into the garden, and it was the garden at the end of the alley by the gas lamp. I had walked into the books.

It wasn't a very big garden and it was full. I'd never seen a garden with so much in it, and all of it high. You couldn't see for more than a couple of metres before the path turned and there were plants leaping out at you from all sides, with long tough stems and big leaves. Given a bit more space it could have become a rain forest, like the garden in the books, which was never the same garden; sometimes it was walled and enclosed, sometimes huge and landscaped, once there were statues and fountains, and once there was a second gate which led into wild countryside—it all depended on who found it each time, and what they were thinking of.

Halfway down the path was an arch with some kind of creeper trained over it, and beyond that something that only rarely appeared in the books—vegetables. Once they had found the remains of a kitchen garden with cold frames and cloches and old rhubarb bells, but never anything like this, rows of runner beans and cabbages and onions. A head rose up from behind some raspberry canes and said, 'James, I think your visitor is here.'

Another head appeared, looming out like the green man from among the runner beans; Mr and Mrs Rudd. And they said, both at once, 'Hullo, Bridget.'

'We've been rehearsing,' said Mrs Rudd, standing up. She was wearing nice old gardening clothes and wellies and when I saw her I thought, everyone should have a mother like that, even though there is nothing wrong with mine, nothing at all. I knew why I thought it, too, as soon as I'd finished thinking it. She was like one of the mothers in her husband's books and then I thought, How did he know she would end up like that when he married her?

The other head had gone back into the runner beans and the owner was crashing about inside. Mrs Rudd came towards me, wiping her hands on her sacking apron, just as I'd thought she would.

'He'll find his way out in a minute,' she said. 'Would you like a drink?'

I said I would, please. I said I hoped I wasn't disturbing them.

'Not at all,' she said, and as she went past she whispered, 'You're our first fan. James has had letters, of course—well, he used to—but no one ever came here before. He's awfully pleased.'

After that I expected something quite pathetic to shamble out of the runner beans, but at last he emerged looking perfectly cheerful, a medium-sized man with a tidy black and grey beard, carrying the runners in a garden riddle.

He shook my hand. 'How nice to meet you,' he said. 'I thought we might stay out here as it's so fine. Is that all right? You haven't brought a tape recorder to plug in?'

'Oh, no.' It hadn't crossed my mind to do anything so professional, and it did seem a bit sneaky, even if it was the professional way. I followed him past the bean rows and right at the end of the garden where most people have the compost heap, was a little grassy patch with some white iron chairs and a table. Mrs Rudd came back with *beer*. I'd been expecting a cup of tea.

'Is beer all right?' she asked, anxiously, when she saw me staring at it. 'Perhaps you don't . . .'

'Oh, I do,' I said firmly, although not at home, officially.

'I'll leave you to it then,' she said and went back to doing something strenuous among the raspberry canes.

'That's a very business-like clip board,' James Rudd said. 'Are you going to fire questions at me?'

Well, I had been going to, but sitting there in the garden with the beer, I didn't want to do that at all. 'Can we just talk?' I said. 'About the books.'

'Yes,' he said, 'but start with a question or we'll never get started at all. I haven't done this before.'

'Didn't people want to talk about them when you wrote them?'

'I was never very famous,' he said, 'in fact I wasn't famous at all and anyway, it was quite a while ago. I wrote the first one in 1970. Writers didn't go into schools much, or run workshops in those days. Meg and Katy—my two—seem to have a different author every term. I never did anything like that. I just sat at home and wrote books.'

'Did you want to be a writer when you were at school?' That was one of the questions we all asked.

'No, I wanted to be an architect.'

'Are you?' I said, rather abruptly.

'What?'

'Are you an architect?'

'No. I got sidetracked.' He smiled, inside the beard. 'I run a printing firm—not a big commercial press. We do leaflets, letterheads, catalogues, posters—you name it. We're in Bank Street; you know. We call ourselves Foolscap.'

'Why?' I do know it. My sister had her wedding invitations done there. They did them nicely, too.

'It was a size of paper, before we went metric, named after a watermark—are you writing all this down? It's not important.'

'Yes it is. I want to write about you as well as the books. It's meant to be an in-depth study.'

'Ah, I know the kind of thing: "Hairy Mr Rudd told me over a pint of beer . . ."'

'I'll just mention it,' I said.

'The beer?'

'I haven't done this kind of thing before, either,' I told

him. I looked at my list of questions. 'Why did you start writing—if you were a printer, that is? Was it seeing other people's books all the time made you want to try?'

'No, I told you, we don't print books, and this was long before the printing business. I was still trying to be an architect. Why *did* I start?' He seemed to be asking himself. 'I suppose I thought I had a story to tell.'

'And why did you stop?'

'That's what you really want to know, isn't it?'

'Yes,' I said. 'I mean, it wasn't that you suddenly found you couldn't do it any more, was it?'

'Oh no, I could do it.'

'Didn't they sell?'

'Modestly, but if I'd really been a writer I'd have gone on anyway, even if I hadn't been published. You know how it is—how it's meant to be; tormented genius, business goes to pot, starving chidren, wife on the streets, mistresses . . . sorry. You won't get away with that for GCSE, will you? No, I finished the third book—what's it called—?'

I was shocked. He'd forgotten the name of his own book. '*Off the Map*,' I said.

'That's it. Well, I'd finished it, and my editor said, "Right, that's your trilogy out of the way, what next?" and I realized that there *was* nothing next. I'd had a story to tell and I'd told it. That was it. Kaput.'

'What about the book of architects?'

'Speaks for itself, really, doesn't it? My lost career—no, don't try to look sympathetic. I hated being an architect. I knew that before I'd even finished at college. I wrote it to help out a friend; brilliant historian; writes like a ten-year-old. He just can't string a sentence together.'

We didn't seem to be getting far. 'Where were you at college?' I asked, briskly.

'It was an art school,' he said. 'At the time we were just one of the departments. The Faculty of Architecture, we called ourselves—very grand. It was a row of Nissen huts across the car park from the Graphic Design Department, and we shared a canteen with the art students. We thought they were a very low-class bunch.'

'Were they?'

'Not at all. They just didn't bother to try and look respectable while they were working. Some of *us*, I'm afraid, wore suits. We all went to each other's parties and nicked each other's girl friends . . . It was one of the artists, I think, who made me realize why I'd come to the end of my story—yes—it *was* him. How extraordinary.'

'What was?'

'All these years and I've only just realized what he did. He was working at book illustration by then, and he'd come across *Off the Map* at my publishers, and followed it up and got in touch with me. We hadn't met for about five years, right out of touch. Well, I went to see him, and we chewed the fat and I looked at his work, and in his studio I found his sketch book—one of his sketch books. He must have filled dozens, but this was from his final year. It was my final year, too, and in it there was this litle pen and ink drawing of three people sitting on a bashed up sofa on a traffic island. And I looked at it and I said, "My God, the travelling settee!"'

I just looked expectant. He was off; I didn't want to say anything to make him dry up again.

'I said, "Did you do any others?" and he said no, that was the only one. But it was enough. I'd forgotten about the travelling settee till that moment; then it all came back.

'It wasn't a residential college. Most of the students lived at home and came into the city by bus or train, but some of us had bedsits and a few lived in flats. I shared a mouldy basement with three other guys, down near the station, and just up the road from us was an auctioneer's. We used to go up there sometimes and see if there were any job lots worth bidding for—we always needed household goods. Occasionally there would be something so awful that it would be shoved out on to the pavement for the council to dispose of, and one evening two of us were walking home from the pub when we saw this settee dumped in front of the auction room. You could see why no one had bid for it. It wasn't old, not very old, not antique; it was just horrible, covered in a kind of mangy brown plush with orange seat cushions. And two of the castors had come off. One of them had been replaced with a wheel off something else, and someone had tried a kind of field surgery on the offside hind leg and driven in a six inch nail.

'Alan, he was the fellow with me, sat down on it and bounced about a bit, and said, wasn't it just what we could do with? I wasn't too sure, myself, I thought that looking at such a monstrosity every evening could give you bad dreams, but we did need a settee—*something* to sit on. We'd had a party the week before and someone had lit a fire in our sofa. I said they were a low class lot, didn't I? He was trying to cook sausages over it.

' "See what the others think," I said, so we left it there and went back to the flat.

'We didn't have house meetings or anything formal

like that, but when the others got home, about midnight, we described it to them. I said it appeared to have been owned by a left-handed smoker with a limp wrist because the left arm was covered in cigarette burns, and added that he probably spent many days off work each year with unidentified back pains. Alan just said that there was room to sleep on it and that was enough to decide in its favour. We were short of beds. So we agreed that we'd all go down and look at it in the morning before taking a final vote, but I was pretty sure I'd be outnumbered, even though the others might have second thoughts when they saw the ghastly thing. It was,' said James Rudd, 'the most repulsive piece of furniture I'd ever seen. There was actually some form of vegetable growth between the cushions.'

'Oh!' I said. 'Mr McEnery in *Just Down the Street*. The man who grew mushrooms on a mattress.'

'Could well be,' James Rudd said, but he didn't seem very certain. 'Next morning we all went along to the auction rooms, but as soon as we were out of the gate we could see that the settee had gone. I was quite relieved, myself, but Alan was furious. "I expect the dustmen took it," I said. Alan insisted that someone had got up early and crept out ahead of us to swipe the settee. Personally I couldn't imagine anyone going to such lengths for anything so nasty, but the settee had gone and there was nothing to be done about it—fortunately.

'It was the following evening before I found out *where* it had gone. I took a short cut back from college, after a late class, through the coal yard behind the sidings, and there was the settee, parked between two piles of coke. I could see how it had got there because of the tracks in the coal dust; three wheels and the six inch nail. Against my better judgement I told Alan when I got back. "Right," he said. "We'll go out after supper and get it."

'"Suppose the others don't like it after all?" I said. "I don't care," said Alan, "we're not letting it go this time." "Perhaps the men at the coal yard want it?" I said. "They got it first."

'"Probably kids fooling around," Alan snarled. He really did seem to have set his heart on that settee. But the others didn't come home that night. Owing to the acute bed shortage they spent a lot of time on other people's floors and in other people's baths. Officially they weren't supposed to be in our flat at all. We'd sublet, to raise the money for food. So when they hadn't come back by Saturday morning Alan and I went round to the coal yard on our own. And it had gone. You knew I was going to say that, didn't you?'

I hadn't known. I was listening to a story. I didn't want to guess what would happen next, I wanted to hear it being told.

'At first Alan thought I'd been kidding him along, but I showed him the tracks in the coal dust and he had to believe me. Moreover, you could see where the settee had stood because the tracks led away from the place where I'd seen it, between the coke stacks and out towards the Thanet Road. "Right," says Alan, "let's follow it."

'I'd been hoping that the settee, having had a head start, would have got clean away, but as we came out of the coal yard on to the Thanet Road, I spotted it standing on the corner outside the Plasterer's Arms. It was surrounded by children, five of them creeping up on it and three defending it and, I was pleased to note, it was getting severely hacked about. Alan—anyone would have thought it was *his* settee—charged across the road yelling "Oi! Gerroff!" He must have thought they'd all scatter in terror, but most of them just went on bashing each other and the biggest said "Whyyyyyy?"

'"Because it's ours," Alan said. In our household Alan was the arch slob, the tearaway, changed his socks once a month when they stuck to his shoes and claimed he was a socialist anarchist. Now he sounded like a headmaster, but this lad ate headmasters for breakfast. "Why was it in the coal yard, then?"

'"Didn't *you* put it there?" I asked, giving the game away. "How could we put it there if it was yours?" says Ghengis Khan junior, and went back to beating his friend over the head with a fencing stake.

'"Let's come back for it later," I said, not wanting to take on the whole mob, so we walked manfully away while they all jeered, and went to the pub. We ought to have gone to the Plasterer's Arms, to be on the spot, but we were meeting some friends, and when we came back—you know what's coming, of course?'

'It had moved again?'

'Not a trace of it—literally. The first thing I looked for was the track of the six inch nail, but they must have carried it; eight of them could have managed it easily. I wasn't sorry and hoped we'd seen the last of the settee, but of course we hadn't. The next time I came across it it was standing on the grass verge at a corner near the front entrance of the art school. It looked as if it had been the scene of several more battles. The fabric had been ripped off the back and one of the cushions was gone, and there were springs sticking out. The principal of the college was a hard-eyed Scot, and suspected horseplay. Were we responsible? No, we were not. Overnight it shifted again, a little way up the road to the traffic island at the next intersection. We were on our way to the pub when we found it; that was when my friend did the drawing, me, Alan and an art student called Althea. I remember her because she and Alan got very friendly that night and agreed to meet again the following evening.

'"Where?" said Althea.

'"Oh, at the settee," said Alan. That was what started it, really. Because, naturally, the following evening the settee had gone elsewhere, but Alan didn't know where Althea lived and she didn't know where Alan lived, so they had to find it. We finally located it down a side street by the main Post Office, and Althea was there before us. After that it became a routine; "See you at the settee." After all, it never went far, and wherever it went it left that trail behind it where the nail dug into the pavement.'

All the time he was telling me this I was watching James Rudd. Remembering the settee seemed to make him melancholy, in a pleasant sort of way. I hadn't written anything down for a long time.

'It stuck in an alley near the cathedral for a couple of nights and we wondered if it would break the rules if we moved it ourselves. After all, the joy of the thing was not knowing where it would turn up next; the fear that the authorities would remove it, but I suppose they could never catch up with it. Some irate shopkeeper would complain that the settee was obstructing his entrance or obscuring his window, no doubt, but by the time the dustmen arrived the settee had moved on. It had the sense not to go into the cathedral precinct—it wouldn't have lasted long in there—but it went all the way up Haymarket, stopped three days in the car park and one night at the war memorial, and then began a circuit of the city wall. "Anyone seen the settee?" we'd ask. It became a kind of rallying cry. More and more people joined in. Sometimes there'd be twenty of us gathered round it and I began to wonder how much longer it could go on. It was so silly, and so nice . . . it had to stop; and I'd noticed something.'

He paused.

'It was disintegrating?' I said.

'Oh, it was certainly doing that,' he said. 'By now it was down to the frame, one cushion and a few rags of upholstery. No, one night it made a decisive move. It turned into a street that led to the bypass. The settee was leaving town.'

'What happened?' I said; 'when it reached the bypass?'

'I don't know. I lost sight of it. It was the end of term, you see, and it was the final year for all of us at the flat. We were packing up, moving away, most of us never met again. The last—no, the next to last time I saw it, it was standing at the end of a cul-de-sac, quite near the bypass, under a street light, the old-fashioned kind that used to run on gas. I was on my bike, didn't stop, just wondered briefly if I'd ever meet anyone at the settee again and rode on.'

'And did you? Ever meet at the settee again, I mean?'

'No. A few days later I left the place for good, by train, and when we were a couple of minutes from the station I sat forward for a last look at the city and the cathedral, because there was a view across the fields, just before the line went under the bypass. After that you couldn't see anything. And I didn't get my last sight of the cathedral because under the bridge was the settee, standing beside the track like a bench in a park. I felt like crying. It seemed to sum up all the happiness of those last few weeks. You can be terribly sentimental at that age,' he said, and smiled at me. 'You have that pleasure to come. It *is* a pleasure, believe it or not.'

'Was that the end of it?'

'Just a vague memory that faded completely—until I saw my friend's sketch book years later, and then it all came back and I understood where the books had come from.'

'But you said—just now—you'd only just realized what he'd done.'

'Oh yes; because he told me at last what happened to the settee afterwards. A few nights later somebody wedged it across the railway line and derailed a train. No one was killed; I think it was a milk train, something slow, but afterwards, after I knew, I kept thinking, what a lousy thing to do; what a lousy thing, that is, to do with our settee. But now, you see, I knew how the story ended. That's what he did, my friend, quite innocently. He made me understand that I had nothing more to write. You must have realized . . . I mean, you're not going to ask me where I get my ideas from, are you? You know now, don't you?'

'Yes.'

'Well, I knew then that there weren't going to be any more ideas. Either I'd go on writing the same thing over and over again, or I'd stop. So I stopped. But it's taken me eighteen years to see that. Thank you.'

We chatted a bit more and finished the beer. I asked him the rest of the questions, although not the one about where he got his ideas from. And then Mrs Rudd came back and we all said goodbye and I walked home across the allotments. I felt very mournful, just as he had described, thinking about the travelling settee and how happy they had all been because they knew it wouldn't last. I wondered if any of the others had remembered it too, or if James Rudd had been the only one who cared, cared so much that he wrote three books about it.

Though, obviously, the books aren't about a settee. The first one was *Just Down the Street*, then *Over the Wall* and the last one was *Off the Map*. They are about three friends who are coming home from school one day when they take a short cut down an alley they haven't noticed before, and find a gate into a garden, and they love it, although they think they're probably tresspassing, and decide to meet there again the following evening. But they can't find the alley again, or the garden, not for a long while, until they come across it by accident, only it's a different garden, things have changed. Each of the books is about a different person, but they are always looking for the alley that leads to the garden, and as the books go on, and they get older, it gets harder and harder to find because the alley is never in the same place twice, and by the end of the last book they've more or less given up trying to find it, just hope that perhaps . . . one day . . . by chance . . . When I was little I could never quite understand why they gave up looking for the garden; now I could see how sad it was that they knew they didn't need it any more. And I wondered what James Rudd would have written next if he hadn't found out just in time what had happened to the travelling settee, but I guessed that he was glad that he stopped when he did. You have to know when to let go.

2

Too Old to Rock and Roll

'I think it might clear the air,' Valerie said, 'if you called a halt to the ongoing tit-for-tat situation.'

'It's not tit-for-tat.'

'All right, *quid pro quo*.'

'What's that?'

'Up market tit-for-tat. But why not just lay off each other for a bit?'

'He started it,' Greg said. 'He shouldn't have called me a pimplie.'

'And you shouldn't have called him a wrinklie.'

'That's different. It's a sort of general term for anyone over—over—'

'Twenty-five? No need to be tactful,' said Valerie, forty if a day. 'Anyway, it makes no difference whether it's general or not, it still hurts.'

'It's only a joke.'

'If that's only a joke, so is pimplie. Added to which,' Valerie said, 'pimples go away, wrinkles don't.'

'He's not all *that* wrinkled.'

'Quite. And I suppose it was you who stuck that advert for the hair replacement therapy on the fridge.'

'He's always going on about *my* hair.'

'Call a truce,' Valerie said. 'It's very tedious listening to you two sparring all the time.'

'We need a referee,' Greg muttered.

'I know.' Valerie's voice softened. 'Well, anyway, I'll be round at eight. See you then, OK?'

He hung up and went into the kitchen. Valerie didn't miss a thing. It was only on Sunday that he had cut the advertisement for the Hogarth Hair Clinic out of *The Observer* and attached it to the side of the fridge with a magnet; the side that you saw first as you came in from the hall, along with cards for dental appointments and taxis, and the recipe in Mum's handwriting for avocado and chicken soup. It was half hidden under the bus timetable and Dad had missed it. Perhaps it was the only thing of Mum's left in the house, apart from the Christmas tree baubles. Greg slid it further under the timetable and looked at the clipping about the clinic. It advertised a new and revolutionary method of replacing lost growth—of hair, presumably, although it was too coy to come right out and say so—and showed a man's head, seen from above, on which growth had receded to a dim fringe around the ears, and next to it another picture of the same man, youthful and beaming and thatched like a yeti. Clients were advised to telephone the clinic for an appointment with the consultant trichologist before committing themselves to the course of treatment.

Greg could not really imagine his father slogging up to London regularly, not even for the initial appointment with the trichologist. In any case, his hair loss was nothing like so drastic as that threadbare dome in the picture. Standing up and walking about Dad appeared to have a full head of hair, short but flourishing. It was only when seen from above, as Greg had discovered coming downstairs while Dad was on the phone in the hall, that the thinning patch on the crown was noticeable. Subsequently he had made one or two discreet surveys in passing, while Dad was watching television or sitting at table, and realized that Dad had been already alerted to the problem, by his hairdresser, most likely. The latest cut had the look of skilful topiary, every hair arranged to earn its place in the design. The advert on the fridge was intended more as a friendly hint than an insult, although Dad had not shown any signs of taking it either way. It had been there for three days and not a word spoken about it.

Still, Greg supposed, it was an optimistic omen, that hair cut, a sign that Dad was at last sitting up and taking notice. To be fair, he had been sitting up, as it were, for some time. The terrible paralysis that had struck him after Mum died had worn off after about four months, just in time for Christmas. It had been painful, Greg remembered, watching him constantly as he made himself get up, made himself read the paper, cut the hedge, cook a meal. What he had not seen, could only guess at, was Dad at work. In all that time he had driven off every morning, and driven himself through the day, doing whatever needed to be done, presenting a normal front to members of the public, presumably, and then coming home on autopilot and apparently operating on remote control for the rest of the evening. Somewhere inside that programmed android was Stephen Barber, reduced to a micro-chip that controlled the organism; the memory bank that directed the program. At work, Greg supposed, the routine had continued as usual; people came away with new glasses, contact lenses; no one was made blind. It hadn't functioned so well at home. The memory bank knew how to organize an optician, but not a single parent. Half of the working parts was missing.

That things were getting back to normal was due to Valerie. It was Valerie who had been there, entirely by chance, when the unhappy policeman had called to report the accident. Greg could no longer remember why she had been there; they knew her only slightly and it was Mum she had come to see, arriving at just around the time Greg and Dad had been starting to look at the clock and wonder why. She lived about thirty miles away, had a home of her own to go back to, cats to feed, plants to water, a theatre ticket in her purse for the following evening, but when the policeman had offered to drive them to the hospital Dad had turned to this virtual stranger and said, 'Please stay,' and so she had been there when they had returned, making, as Greg guessed later, a series of efficient phone calls back home; had remained until the life support system was switched off—that had been the worst day—and withdrew tactfully for the funeral when the house had been filled with proprietorial Smiths and Barbers.

It was Valerie who had caused Christmas to happen. Greg himself had said nothing about it but Valerie's sensitive antennae had picked up the vibrations and for once she had abandoned tact.

'For Christ's sake, Steve!' he had heard her explode, down in the kitchen, 'what about Greg?'

'He isn't interested in Christmas,' Dad had said, in that heavy, dazed monotone. 'How could he be? Frances *was* Christmas. She made it her own.'

'I'll tell you what,' Valerie said, brutally, 'Frances must

be spinning in her grave to see what a pig's ear you've made of surviving without her.'

His father had gasped, audibly. 'What an appalling thing to say.'

'Why, because she *is* in her grave? Mourning her is one thing—but for how long? There's a lot to be said for an official period, after which you throw off your black crêpe and get back to normal. This is the rest of your life, Steve. It's the rest of Greg's life. Who do you think you are, Queen Victoria?'

'It's only four months.'

'It's at *least* four months. If Christmas with Frances was so wonderful isn't it worth trying to keep it going? It was wonderful because she enjoyed it. It wasn't a chore to her, no nonsense about only doing it for the children. She enjoyed making it good for the three of you. How do you think she'd feel if you cared so little—?'

'I care so much.'

'—cared so little that you couldn't try to keep alive what she began.'

'Christmas or Greg?'

'Good God, you made a joke,' Valerie said.

Greg cornered her later while Dad went round to the off licence.

'Are you coming here for Christmas?'

Valerie looked at him sharply.

'Christmas? What made you think that?'

'It's the thirtieth of November,' Greg said. 'Isn't that time to be thinking of Christmas?'

'I usually visit my parents,' Valerie said.

'They won't miss you just for once, will they?'

'I should think they might, actually.'

'So would we,' Greg said. He did not mean to be manipulative, but he knew that Valerie *must* be made to stay, because if this Christmas didn't happen, there might never be a Christmas again.

'Did you have a very special time?' Valerie asked, gently.

'We did it our own way,' Greg said. 'Mum's way. She hated Christmas beginning too soon, you know, cards in the shops in September and Santa's Grotto at Hallowe'en. We never did anything till December the first, with the Advent calendar, then we used to send our cards, but we never put up decorations or dressed the tree till a week before Christmas. We usually did it on the evening after school broke up. We did it together.'

'The three of you?'

'No, just me and her. Dad put the holly and stuff up. The decorations are in a hat box—it was my great grandmother's—I used to get them out one at a time, and Mum would tell me where they came from. The first year they had their own home, and we were really hard up, Mum got a little tree—I thought it was huge because it was as tall as me—I was three, that's how little it was—she couldn't afford any decorations, and then she found this cornflakes box in the loft that had got left behind when the last people moved out, and there was all this tinsel in it, and some tree decorations. So she used them, and after that, every year, she'd buy some more, just two or three each time, but she still kept those first ones. Not the tinsel, you know how tinsel goes when it's old, but the baubles. They got broken, bit by bit, they were that very thin glass stuff, you know; but we've still got one of them. It looks a bit scruffy now, all the colour's come off, but we still use it. We always hang it up first of all. I've got the box in my room.'

He had put it there when Dad started clearing everything out; clothes, jewellery, books, letters, and he had been wondering how and when to produce it. Now he knew.

'You *must* come,' he said to Valerie.

'If I'm asked.'

'I'm asking.'

'We'll have to work on it,' Valerie said.

'Won't one of your neighbours feed the cats?'

'I wasn't thinking of the cats.' Valerie, sitting at the kitchen table competently slicing onions for spaghetti Bolognese, had paused and looked straight at him.

'It'll be hard work, Greg. We almost left it too late.'

'For Christmas?'

'For Steve. Perhaps we've been soft-pedalling for too long. I don't know if you heard us just now—yes, you did, of course you did—well, I said something really unkind, something I wouldn't have dreamed of saying normally, and he actually snapped at me; answered back. That's the first time I've seen any signs of animation since Frances died.

'I've been admiring you, Greg, for the way you've coped—coped with Steve, as much as anything. And I suddenly thought, Dammit, I like this man. I don't want to feel sorry for him, I want to admire him, too, so I said . . . what I did say, and I think it worked. This is a shocking thing to suggest to a respectable teenager, but Greg, I think you might try being a little ruder, now and again. Be a bit selfish.'

'Cruel to be kind?'

'Yes—but not too cruel.'

Had he been too cruel? It was past Easter now, the tree decorations long back in their box, the presents tarnished with familiarity, the tree itself still moulting brown spines at the end of the garden.

He had waited until Christmas Eve before taking Valerie's advice, keenly observing the situation, calculating the optimum moment to slip his stiletto between the armour plating, then standing back, breathless, to discover whether he had lanced a boil or punctured a vital organ.

In the afternoon when Dad came home from a solitary tour of the supermarket and before Valerie arrived from Ipswich, he had dug out the hat box from where he had buried it at the bottom of the wardrobe, and clattered *cheerfully* downstairs with the box under his arm. His father looked out of the kitchen doorway, haggard, sunken-eyed, stooped.

'What have you got there?'

Greg raised the box like a trophy.

'The tree decorations.'

Dad had advanced from the doorway with something like rage in his eyes.

'Where did you find them?'

'Didn't find them,' Greg said, pertly, over his shoulder, and went into the living room. 'I hid them in the wardrobe. Didn't want you throwing *them* out.'

Dad followed him into the undecorated, unheated room. 'Why have you brought them down?'

'To put on the tree.'

'What tree? We aren't having a tree. How could you—'

'*I* want a tree,' Greg said, baldly. 'Mum wouldn't have wanted to spoil my Christmas.' That was when he had paused, waiting to see what effect his effrontery would have. His father stood looking round slowly, seeming to awake to something he had not seen before, at Greg, and away again, then at his watch.

'It's too late to get a tree now,' he said, hopelessly.

'Valerie's bringing it with her,' Greg said, 'and some holly. Shall I light the fire?'

After that it had been easier; the occasional back-chat, a light-hearted insult, a show of the ill temper he had been carefully, fearfully, suppressing for so long, until they were sniping regularly, amicably, as they had always done. And Valerie, after that Christmas visit, came more often, stayed longer, until the spare room became known as Valerie's room. No one else wanted to use it.

But had he gone too far with the Hogarth Hair Clinic advertisement? Repeated gibes about flares and ageing trendies had finally provoked Dad into going out and buying some new clothes to replace the disintegrating favourites that Mum had chosen for him, but anyone, at any age, needed new clothes from time to time. Suggesting that somebody needed new hair was near unforgiveable.

Greg lifted the magnet and slid out the offending square of newsprint, screwed it into a ball and chucked it into the swing bin. He moved the magnet round to the door of the fridge, which was the place for messages, slipped a sheet of paper under it and wrote in violent and unmissable green felt tip:

GONE TO BAND PRACTICE. VAL RANG.
WILL BE HERE AT EIGHT.

Then he put the casserole in the oven, turned on the gas, mark 2, and went to check that the table was properly laid in the dining room. It was his pleasure now to know that when Valerie arrived it would be to a table exquisitely prepared, white napkins, gleaming glassware, flowers and candles, and to Dad, who would have had an hour or so to prepare himself exquisitely instead of batting distractedly round the kitchen dropping grease and bean sprouts, before dropping a charred pie dish on the table and ripping off sheets of kitchen roll because the napkins hadn't been washed from last time. When Greg came home at nine they would be sitting relaxed in the front room, pleasantly boozed up and ready to eat the meal that awaited only Greg's last loving attentions before appearing on the table along with hot rolls, butter pats, green salad and a nice red wine, properly *chambré*. At the front door he paused to switch on the porch light in readiness, and looked back to make sure that nothing was out of place. He hated to acknowledge it—and Dad never would, but even Mum had never been this well organized.

The band practices took place at Mark's house because Mark's house was detached and both his parents worked late shifts, but principally because Mark was the drummer and the least mobile. Greg was the roadie, which meant, since none of them was old enough to drive, that when they played a gig he was responsible for loading all the equipment and the drums on to Mark's father's trailer and hauling it through the streets to the Co-op Hall or the room over the Prince of Wales. Toby, the lead guitarist, had lettered a banner with the band's name, MEANS TEST, long enough to tack round three sides of the trailer.

The band was high minded and accepted only politically correct engagements; Rock Against Racism, Rock Against the Poll Tax and Rock on behalf of anyone who happened to be on strike. Toby was a tireless monitor of Trade Union discontent and made forecasts, sometimes months in advance, of who was likely to come out next. Toby's father was a Conservative councillor, but permissibly wet. Greg occasionally suspected that he himself had been admitted to Means Test solely on the grounds that his old man had been seen on the streets, canvassing for Labour at the last election. As roadie he had little to do on practice nights unless Morris, the bass guitarist, had had an asthma attack, but he had joined them in the New Year as much to establish a reason for going out as a need to make music.

'Music?' Dad said, morosely, 'or Rock and Roll?'

'Rock, not Roll,' Greg had said, daring him to imply that wanting to play in a rock band so soon—five months, by then—was unfeeling, unseemly, unfilial. But Dad had said nothing about that, had said only, 'Had a good time?' when he returned and had thereafter refrained from comment when he started playing records again, up in the bedroom.

When the practice ended, just before nine, Mark produced cans of lager from the fridge, Morris said he had enough blow for one roll-up and Means Test settled in for a dissolute evening. Greg made his excuses and left.

'Want to get back and catch them at it?' Toby inquired as he went out, but no, that was not what he wanted at all. He wanted to be at home, opening the back door to an odour of hot, cooked food, to hear contented voices from the living room, to take a beer and go in and join them for half an hour before they all sat down to his casserole and he could enjoy Valerie's compliments about his cooking and his table laying. He said nothing of this, however. Wanting to be cosy at home was not part of the Rock ethos.

'Got an assignment to finish,' he said, and departed in a chorus of friendly groans.

The light was on in the living room when he approached the house. Dad was standing in there alone, his back to the window, but Valerie's car was in the drive; she must have left the room for something. As Greg opened the gate he saw her through the dappled glass of the front door, advancing down the lighted hall and turning right into the living room. And as she did, his father left the window and moved forward, his arms held wide. Greg proceeded to the back door very slowly. The last thing he wanted to do was catch them at it and spoil everything.

He could hardly take the credit for having made it happen, but he had done all he could to help things along, making sure that Valerie knew she was welcomed by at least one member of the household, even in the worst days when Dad had wanted to see no one; making sure that Dad knew how much he liked Valerie. He was in no hurry. He was not keen for either of them to think that he wanted to replace Mum, that he had forgotten her already, that he did not miss her constantly to the extent that when he saw the house in his mind's eye she was always in it. He still expected to see her in the garden, he still did see her out shopping, in cars, on a bus, her very self, until the features inevitably dissolved into someone else, someone who did not resemble her at all. But he was sure that Valerie never supposed for one moment that he had forgotten. And Dad had never shown signs of understanding that he felt anything at all.

When he went into the front room they were sitting down again, either side of the unlit fire. On the hearth was a big earthenware jar that Mum had found in an Oxfam shop, filled with tulips, red, pink, orange, yellow; all the colours of flame, blazing coolly.

'Valerie brought them,' Dad said, and Greg saw that he was smiling, a real, effortless smile, not the miserable rictus he had forced in company as though taught how to do it by a physiotherapist. Greg had seen Valerie's garden, compact and brilliant inside its trellised walls, like a box of flowers behind her ground floor flat. The three cats had lain in the spring sunshine on a lawn the size and texture of a carpet. Even in March the French doors had stood open to the sheltered air. Would Valerie want to leave all that?

He looked at her, smiling back at Dad. Was she *expecting* some reward for her kindness, for her devotion to two near strangers, the husband and son of a friend, or had she considered it a moral duty, or had she just seen that it needed doing and done it, and was now taking pleasure purely in her success? Then he looked again at Dad; something was different, something had changed, not just the smile and the haircut, there was something else that he had seen without really noticing, when he saw Dad in the window. It was his clothes, a new black sweater over a striped shirt, and *jeans*. His father was wearing jeans.

'I thought it was time I had some new gear,' Dad said, looking almost sheepish, but mostly pleased with himself—for the effort rather than the effect, Greg thought. 'I can't go on shaming you in public.'

Wow! Sarcasm. Was it just possible that everything was going back to normal, that the man sitting there by the fireside was slowly being transformed back into Stephen Barber, the humorous, handsome man he had grown up with, the man who had married Mum—was he coming home again?

'Do you want a drink?' Valerie asked him, 'or are you ready for us to eat? Your casserole smells wonderful.' She said nothing about Dad's new turn-out, but there was no need to say anything. Each knew how pleased and relieved the other was.

At dinner Dad was more than courteous, courtly, almost, as if trying to make a good impression, seeing Valerie for the first time, or for the first time as a woman, at any rate.

Toby had been very wide of the mark in his assumption that Dad and Valerie were having it off. This was the first time that Greg had seen him deliberately aiming to please her, to attract her attention. Once he would not have had to try. Women had been charmed by him simply because he was there. Greg recalled dropping in at the optician's on the way home from school, because it had looked empty of customers and he fancied a chat. The two lady assistants had seemed resentful and embarrassed, Dad awkward, not quite himself.

Mum had laughed when he told her. 'Don't for God's sake do that again. They both flirt like mad with him and they're insanely jealous of each other.'

‘What about you?’ he’d asked, indignantly.

‘Me? They probably think I don’t understand him and ruined his life. I expect they secretly pray that I’ll fall under a bus.’

He’d forgotten that crack. It hadn’t been a bus, in the event. Her car had collided with a blameless milk float, an accident seemingly so slight that it was difficult to take it seriously, hard to believe that someone had died in it. He sometimes wondered what the two jealous women in the shop had thought. He remembered their wreath; chrysanthemums. What *had* they thought? Had they privately begun to hope?

They were both young and quite pretty; Yvonne and Denise, and then there was Mary Dane who came in on Wednesday afternoons, and, of cours~ Susannah, Mrs Shannon, who was the other optician. What *had* they all thought, wondered, hoped? What would they think if they could see Valerie, who was not very young or very pretty—but right, absolutely right.

‘I’ll wash up,’ he said.

‘Oh no, that’s not fair,’ Valerie protested. ‘You cooked it all.’

‘I’ve started so I’ll finish,’ he said. ‘You go and sit in the other room.’

‘We’ll wash up together,’ Dad said, managing to make it sound like a long-promised treat, so Greg went upstairs, left his door ajar, and listened to them in the kitchen, laughing, talking, late into the night, and then silence.

Next morning he refused to satisfy his curiosity about which room Valerie had slept in, and went out before either of them was up. He helped out at a bakery on

Saturday mornings, from seven o'clock, so there was no question of delivering early morning tea and an awkward juggling of trays while he listened at keyholes.

So, no, he hadn't been too cruel and Valerie had been right. Between them they had jolted Dad back to life, like electrodes applied to a heart that had stopped beating.

During the following week Dad bought some more clothes for both of them. Greg prudently asked for the money and did his own shopping, since Means Test had agreed that they would play in collarless shirts, black trousers and high laced boots. Dad would never have demurred at any of this but he would not have thought of it unprompted although, Greg had to admit, the clothes that he was buying for himself were a lot more fashionable than the things he had worn when Mum was alive. He even stopped wearing a suit to work and went out in a jacket that Greg could imagine himself considering in a year or two. At the weekend, when Valerie came over, they went out on Saturday and Sunday.

'Do you want to come?' Dad said, with what Greg hopefully recognized as a distinct lack of enthusiasm.

'Not with exams coming up,' Greg said virtuously, and from his bedroom window watched them get into the car and drive away. The thinning patch in Dad's hair hardly showed with that new cut, in fact he had been back to the hairdresser since and had some more topiary. When he closed the passenger door for Valerie he *ran* round to the driver's side, slim and agile in his jeans and tailored shirt. Greg normally drew the line at tailored shirts but on Dad they looked good and showed how flat his stomach was. Greg, satisfied, settled down to his revision.

On Wednesday Dad came home earlier than usual.

'Do you mind fending for yourself tonight?' he asked. Greg heard the bath running.

'Going out?'

'A party.'

'A *party*?' Dad at a party? 'Where?'

'Yvonne's getting engaged. You know, Yvonne at the shop.'

Greg had imagined that Yvonne might be getting big ideas, the way Dad was turning out. He had not thought of her having a private life away from the shop, with a family, boy friends.

'Where does she live?'

'Oh, out past the ring road. I've got the address somewhere. I don't suppose I'll be very late but don't wait up.'

'Won't it be a bit of a rave-up?' Greg asked, dubiously. 'I mean, she's only about twenty-something, isn't she?'

'Twenty-six.'

'They'll all be bopping. You won't like the music.'

Dad looked irritated. 'How do you know I won't like the music?'

'You don't like mine,' Greg said.

'Yvonne's friends are likely to be a good bit older than you.'

'And a good bit younger than *you*,' Greg muttered.

'I heard that. Why do you suppose Yvonne invited me?'

'Out of politeness?' Greg suggested. 'You're her boss. I don't expect she thought you'd say yes. Is Valerie going?'

'Valerie? Of course not.'

'She might like to go to a party.'

'Oh, for heaven's sake, she's probably got better things to do. I can't haul her over here for that.'

He bounded upstairs again; bounded. Greg tried to recall if Dad had ever been to a party with Mum; they'd gone out to dinner parties often enough, and evenings spent informally with friends, but never a party, with dancing, with people twenty years younger. It was unhealthy, degrading; no wonder he didn't want Valerie to see him making a fool of himself.

He went out half an hour later, in new shoes. Greg regretted throwing away the advertisement for the Hogarth Hair Clinic. It ought to be right there on the fridge, where he would see it when he came in. He wasted ten minutes searching through the Sunday paper for an ad he remembered seeing about face lifts. It was after midnight when Dad came home.

Valerie arrived as usual on Friday evening. Greg gave Means Test a miss after ringing Morris to make sure that he was in good health, and produced a lavish salad with chilled cucumber soup. When he heard her car pull up on the gravel of the drive he went into the kitchen to prepare the drinks—G and T for Valerie, beer for himself and Scotch on the rocks for Dad—to give Dad a chance to go to the door and enjoy his greeting in private. He opened bottles, cans, poured liquid, dropped in ice cubes, but the door did not open. Instead he heard the bell ring and, when no one responded, went to answer it himself. Once upon a time he had always done this, virtually lying in wait for his first sight of the car coming up the road, but for the last few weeks it had been Dad who lay in wait.

Why didn't the silly sod take his chance now?

Valerie was on the doorstep, overnight bag in one hand, off-licence carrier in the other.

'Hullo, Greg, take the bottles, will you? There's something else in there for you.'

'Thanks—let's have your case.' He ushered her in. 'I don't know where Dad's got to—he was here just now. Go into the front room, I'm just getting your drink.'

'What a good host you are,' Valerie said, surrendering both bags. 'Everyone should have someone like you to come home to.'

The telephone gave a sharp ping. They waited for it to begin ringing.

'Somebody changed their minds?' Valerie said.

'No, Dad must have put the extension down upstairs.'

He went back to the kitchen. The phone was by the bed for emergencies—Mum had been a midwife—but Dad usually made his calls in the hall. Greg emptied the carrier bag; Muscadet in the fridge, they could have that later. Fitou, that would go nicely with his *boeuf bourguignon* tomorrow; and for him? There was something long and slim, wrapped in tissue; a proper cook's knife. Only last week he'd been bitching about the state of the kitchen equipment. He tested the blade; perfect; lethal; he could hardly wait to get at Saturday's beef.

Dad came downstairs at last and went into the front room. Greg decelerated his preparations to give them a decent interval before carrying in the tray. Dad and Valerie were in the right places, and seemed to have been there for some time.

'I was just saying, I shan't be here tomorrow,' Dad was saying.

'Not at all?'

'Oh, I'll be back in the evening, but I'll have to go into the shop.'

'You were in last week . . . weren't you?' Dad took turns with Susannah Shannon to cover Saturdays.

'Yes, but she just rang, she can't make it this week. We'll square it another time. Still, you can entertain each other, can't you?'

'Rather short notice, isn't it?' Greg said, disapprovingly. It was not until later, when he was spooning cream into the cucumber soup, that it occurred to him that no one had rung up. Dad had made the call.

Greg did the washing on Saturday mornings as Mum had always done. Valerie volunteered to prepare a light lunch to keep them going until the *boeuf bourguignon* that evening. Greg, in the hall, looked back at the comfortable sight of her figure bent over the working surface, grating cheese, and nipped upstairs to his father's room; closed the door and rang the optician's.

'May I speak to Mr Barber, please?'

'I'm afraid he's not in today.' Denise had not recognized his voice. 'Would you like to speak to Mrs Shannon or shall I take a message?'

'No, thank you,' Greg said. 'It's personal.'

That would set them wondering, but it was personal. It was. It was.

'See you next week,' Valerie said, on the doorstep, Sunday evening. She was speaking to Greg but it was Dad who answered.

'I'm not sure. Can I ring you?'

'Well—yes, of course;' Valerie sounded faintly surprised. Greg was more than faintly surprised and at the same time, not surprised at all.

'What's happening next week, then?' he said, as the tail lights disappeared at the end of the road. He waved, one last salute as always, but Dad was already back indoors.

'I said, what's happening next week?' He advanced down the hall. 'Where will we be?'

'Here . . . I don't know.' Dad was looking the other way, not at anything, just the other way.

'*I'll* be here.'

'Look, it's not a regular thing, is it?'

'What isn't?'

'Valerie coming here.'

'Yes it is.'

'Well, I might be doing something else next weekend.'

'*What*?'

'What the hell's it got to do with you?'

'I want to see Valerie next weekend.' Greg felt his lip trembling.

'Why don't you go there?'

'She hasn't asked me.'

'I'll ask *her*,' Dad said, brightly, turning. 'She must be sick of trekking over here every week.'

'No she's not.'

'How do you know? Look, it's not—it's—it's unfair to involve someone else too much with our problems.'

'*Problems? Involve?*'

'Valerie's a friend, she's a good friend, she's done so much for us,' Dad was gabbling now, 'but we can't expect her to go on . . . to go on . . .'

'To go on with what?'

'To go on. I mean, she's only a friend.'

'*Only* a friend?' Greg saw the lights come on. 'But I thought you—and her . . .'

'No.'

'What did you expect?' Toby asked, cleaning his fingernails with a plectrum. 'He's free, he's got over your mum, he wants to start again.'

'What about Valerie?'

'Oh, come *on*,' Toby sighed; 'she's too old for him.'

'They're the same age. I asked her.'

'There you are, I've seen her, remember. She looks her age, he doesn't. And he doesn't want to be seen with someone like that. People will think he can't do any better for himself. Poor old Steve, can't pull the birds any more.'

The bird that Dad had pulled was twenty-four and looked eighteen.

'God, aren't you clever. I wish I could cook,' she said, when Greg served a ratatouille on Friday evening.

'Can't you?' he said, chillingly.

Dad looked at her damply and fondled her shoulder.

'I should learn, if I were you,' Greg advised her. 'I shan't always be here.' And neither will you, he added, silently.

3

Front

If you asked anyone today to name the Seven Wonders of the World they would probably start with Disneyland and then stick. When I was at school we knew them all; the pyramids of Egypt, the Pharos of Alexandria, the Temple of Diana at Ephesus, the Statue of Zeus at Olympia, the tomb of Mausolus at Halicarnassus, the Colossus of Rhodes and the Hanging Gardens of Babylon. We also knew that, apart from the pyramids, they no longer existed, so we could only guess at what they had looked like. It struck me that they were certainly huge, and that was why they had been wonderful; early civilizations had been just as prone as we are to admire things because they are enormous; New York's World Trade Centre, the CN Tower in Toronto. All except the Hanging Gardens of Babylon; nothing was said about the size of those and I thought I knew what they looked like, at any rate. They looked like Rockingham Crescent.

The Crescent was a terrace of three-storey houses on top of our hill. We lived five streets down, far enough down for even the attics of The Crescent to be invisible from our attic, and for years I did not know it was there. I heard of it. 'Oh, so-and-so lives in The Crescent,' grown-ups remarked, but so-and-so was never anyone we visited and it was not on the way to any of the places we did visit; school, the shops, the cinema, the park.

Only when I was given a bicycle and went in for uphill endurance tests did I discover that The Crescent was not some distant, unattainable El Dorado but simply the road at the top of the hill.

Purple-faced, standing on the pedals, I did not know I had reached it until, labouring up Stanley Street, I discovered that the road had turned sharp right and levelled out. I dismounted and stayed where I was, leaning on the handlebars, head down, trying to breathe again without being sick. Stanley Street was 1 in 5 and the houses went down in steps, each lower than the last. I'd never noticed this before because, from the corner of our street, which was quite near the bottom, I'd only ever looked up. The Stanley Street houses stopped short of the hill top and on the right was an open grassy space that looked as if it were mown only rarely and ended in an abrupt lip where the hill dropped away below it. On the left was The Crescent—I identified it by the ancient iron street sign—and as soon as I saw it I knew that I had found the Gardens of Babylon.

It was a very shallow curve but it rose up like a cliff face. I had seen cliffs at Dover, white from a distance, but the closer you got, the greyer they seemed, grey and green where vegetation had sprung in cracks and on ledges. The Crescent was the same. The houses were faced with peeling stucco, white, grey, cream, but the stucco was hardly visible for every house was draped in vines; clematis, wisteria, jasmine, rambling roses, ivies and creepers, cascades of greenery, torrents of it, round windows, over doors, down into the areas below the pavement, interrupted here and there by a streak of red or white; a window box or a basket of petunias and pelargoniums. I knew enough about plants to realize that in fact it was all growing *up*, not down, but the impression was of a riotous tumbling; hanging gardens.

It was a summer afternoon. The sun shone full on The Crescent; the air was quite still. So far above the town it was silent, too. The whole place was transfixed, a mirage, until a sudden murmur of wind set every leaf and tendril quivering, as if the entire terrace had unanimously shuddered. Then it was still again.

To think that all this was here, had always been here, not 300 yards from our house. There was no one in the street but me. No one left a house or entered. No face appeared at a window, or hand twitched a curtain; no voice, no music; even the birds that sang sounded very far away. Reluctant to break the enchantment I stayed where I was, still clinging to the handlegrips and gazing up at the hanging gardens, but I knew that somehow I had to leave; I must make myself leave.

My other major birthday present was a wristwatch. I looked at it unwillingly. It was half past three. I was not expected home until five, for tea, and our home was barely one minute away by bike. Almost I was disappointed. I did not want to leave but I wanted to be *forced* to leave, to have to tear myself away and drag home with many a backward glance. Finding that I had no need to go placed me in imminent danger of leaving without regret, of abandoning a place that had ceased to exert any hold over me. But telling myself that my mother would worry that I had been involved in an accident—it was my first day out on wheels—I turned the bicycle with one last lingering look at the hanging gardens, and began to coast back down Stanley Street with a heavy hand on the brake. It was my first experience of courting sorrow.

'I'll come back,' I whispered, 'tomorrow.' But the next day I rode downhill, towards the town, to experiment with danger and traffic lights. I did not go back to The Crescent that day, nor the next. The longer I waited the better it would be when I did; there was always another day, and another. Weeks passed. I did not mention The Crescent to anyone, as if I had been trespassing and needed to conceal the fact, but I thought of it often with a thrill of nostalgia that grew more poignant the longer I stayed away from the austere silence of the hill top, the lush waterfalls of vines. I could have walked there in not much more than five minutes. I did not go back again for three years.

Patricia Coleman and I must have started at the High School the same term, but we were in the second year before we noticed each other and in the third before we became, briefly, friends. There was no reason why we should not have been, but we were in different classes and rarely met. Then, in the third year, we were put in the same set for maths, and sets, like death, cut across class barriers. It was by no means a meeting of twin souls; perhaps one of us loaned the other a protractor or we converged on the pencil sharpener at the same moment. When we found ourselves by chance together in the dinner queue, there was a reason to speak, some general comment on the quality of the food, possibly. At school we talked about the food in the way that adults talk about the weather; something to discuss among people who have nothing at all to say to each other. Eventually we lingered in the cloakroom and talked, until the duty prefect threw us out. That must have been it—the duty prefect's doing. We walked home together. Even so, it was a couple of weeks before we realized how close to each other we lived.

The school was at the south end of the town, on the road that ran straight through it, pausing to become the High Street for a short distance. Just where the shops began, the dry cleaners and newsagents and hairdressers that always seem to congregate and hang about on the approaches to towns, Patricia—it was Pat by now—would slow down and say, 'I turn off, here.' We then hovered on the corner, finishing the conversation which had lasted us from the school gate, something urgent and instantly forgettable, and then Pat would say, 'See you tomorrow,' or, on Fridays, 'See you on Monday,' and strike off to the right up a side street the name of which I never noticed. I assumed that this was the street she lived in. I walked on past the parade of shops, picked up the evening paper at the newsagent's and then I too turned right, up Stanley Street, across the end of Speke Avenue, by the pillar box, and right again into Livingstone Drive, which was ours. In all my life, except for that one voyage of discovery, I had never been further up the hill than Livingstone Drive.

After about a fortnight, as Pat and I stood on the corner taking our customary ten minutes to wind down the conversation, she said, 'Are you expected?'

'Expected where?'

'At home.'

'I am this evening. Mum and Dad are going out and I've got to baby-sit.' My sister was ten; hardly a baby. 'Why?'

'I thought you might like to come home for a bit.'

Of all the things that Pat and I discussed walking back from school, our homes had never been mentioned. The friendship was a school thing, but I suppose we were now sufficiently warmed up to feel a faint curiosity about each other, and to wonder how each would measure up when confronted by the other's family. And so as soon as Pat said 'I thought you might like to come home for a bit,' I glanced involuntarily up that right-hand turning to look properly, for the first time, at the houses which lined it. Disappointingly, reassuringly, they were Victorian terraces, just like ours; red brick, terracotta facings, sash windows, grey slates capped by red ridge tiles, with comforting green and yellow privet hedges and low brick walls bounding the small front gardens. No gates, as in our street, as in most streets in Britain, I guess. The gates had gone in the war, for scrap, along with the iron railing that had once topped the brick walls, sawn off at the ankle leaving blunt black stumps. I should feel at home in such a house. I should not shine, or feel inferior; it was my proper place.

'Tomorrow, then?' Pat said. Tomorrow was Friday. 'Come and have tea.' This too was proper. In those days tea was a meal to be invited to, a meal at a table, with bread and butter.

'Where does she live?' my mother asked, when I said that I would be late home, and why.

'That road up by the fish shop.'

It was actually a fish and chip shop. For a moment I thought the invitation was going to be vetoed. Could one be seen socializing with people who lived in a street with a fish and chip shop on the corner?

'She lives by the *fish* shop?'

'No, further up.' At a respectable distance, I hoped to suggest. After all, my mother could hardly put a whole street out of bounds because of something right at the end of it. There was a pub at the far end of ours.

'Wellesley Road,' my mother said, after thinking for a bit. 'It's quite nice up there. What did you say her name was?'

'Pat Coleman.'

'What does her father do?' This was not quite so snobbish as it sounds. My mother was trying to work out if the name Coleman meant anything to her; was he Coleman the barber, Coleman the bank manager, Coleman the coalman?

'I don't know,' I said. What I did know was that he was never mentioned. Mummy was spoken of a great deal, but not Daddy, although it was somehow understood that he existed. He wasn't dead. A fearful thought suddenly struck me; perhaps he was in gaol; Coleman the burglar. But no, people from Wellesley Road didn't go to prison, any more than they did from Speke Avenue or Livingstone Drive. That kind of thing went on down on the council estate, so I was given to understand, after all, what could you expect . . .?

'Probably in business,' my mother said, comfortingly; comforting herself. Business implied desks, secretaries, filing cabinets and, of course, money. None of this was said. 'Perhaps you could ask her here, some time?'

I should have thought of that. One look at Pat would have reassured her. Pat was the most *medium* person I had ever met. She might have been assembled from a set of statistics; average height, average build, neither fat nor thin, fairish hair, fairish skin; always somewhere around the middle of the class lists, neither embarrassingly stupid nor insultingly clever—like me, really. That is why we were in the same set for maths. In lessons she always answered questions correctly but never volunteered suggestions. She was safe. One look at her, two minutes' conversation, would have told my mother that.

'Be home by six-thirty, then,' she said, 'before it gets dark.' It wouldn't get dark till well after seven, but I inferred that I was being allowed quite desperate licence.

I felt rather daring, on Friday, turning right, past the fish shop, up Wellesley Road with Pat. I was pushing my bike with a text book spread across the handlebars, and we did our homework as we went. Although we were in different sets for French we found that we had been given exactly the same translation. The teacher would not have approved of the way we were doing it, but we gave it our full attention, so we were quite a long way up Wellesley Road before I noticed just how far we had come. I had dropped the French book, stopped while Pat went to pick it up, and looked back. The road had curved considerably, and steeply, and the High Street was out of sight.

'Do you live right at the end?' I said.

'No, round the corner,' Pat said, dusting off the book. I looked up ahead and for the first time saw that we were almost at the end of the road. A few yards on it turned at a sharp angle to the left, and there was nothing in front of us but some scrubby elder bushes and a couple of buddleia. Beyond them was the sky, and I realized that by a circuitous route we had come to the top of the hill, and at the same moment Pat said, 'We live in Rockingham Crescent.'

'Really? Right in it?' I wished I'd known beforehand, so that I could have told my mother, but what I chiefly felt was astonishment. After all these years of promising myself another visit—one day—here I was by chance about to see it again without any planning or forethought. In one minute, in thirty seconds, I should once more set eyes on the hanging gardens, and in the remaining fifteen seconds experienced joyful anticipation and great reluctance, both at the same time. Did I want to return like this, unready, in the wrong frame of mind? What was wrong about it? I felt obscurely that I *should* have prepared myself, but it was too late now, we were at the corner, turning it. Almost unwillingly, I looked.

Nothing had changed. Except that this time I was seeing it from the opposite end, the view was exactly as I remembered it. The houses were a little smaller, perhaps, but all houses were a little smaller, these days, the road narrower, but so was ours, the expanse of grass that faced the houses less green and more littered, but otherwise all, all the same.

The side of the end house was deep in Virginia creeper, just turning red. The autumn sun was soft, slightly hazy, and as before shone full on to the arc of greenery, the hanging gardens. There were fewer baskets and window boxes, in fact there was none, but I put this down to the season. People were planting bulbs in their window boxes now, weren't they? They were in our street.

'Which one's yours?' I said.

'Second one,' Pat said, 'with the red door.' I drew my eyes from the green sweep of The Crescent, which, from where we were walking, was foreshortened into one Niagara of vines, and turned to the house we were approaching. It did not disappoint me. Ivy swarmed over the wall of the area and up the steps to the front door where clematis took over and higher up gave place to the Virginia creeper that had come across from next door and paused to engulf the windows before continuing to the third house and beyond. The windows were so overgrown it was difficult to make out what shape they were, and the ivy had been allowed to crawl across the fanlight over the door. I tried to imagine how it would look from inside, and gave up, knowing that I was about to find out, for Pat was opening the door.

'What about my bike?'

'Oh, put it in the area, it'll be safe,' Pat said. I thought she meant me to take it down the steps to the basement, but there was just room inside the gateless opening to stand a bicycle and a dustbin which was there already, belching richly from under a dented lid tipped on at an angle.

I parked the bike and pushed the lid back into place, meanwhile staring down into the area. What had I expected to see? A kind of plunge pool, perhaps, boiling with leaf and stem. Instead the steps went precipitously down into a sump of old prams, bicycle wheels, two more dustbins, tea chests, lath and plaster—part of a ceiling. Out of it emerged a door under the steps and a cracked window hung with a yellow net curtain and swags of cobweb more substantial than the curtains. A few ferns drooped out of crevices in the wall.

'Come on,' said Pat, in the doorway. I followed her up the steps, but not before I had noticed the area of the next house, almost entirely occupied by a striped mattress.

Now I really was wondering what I should find inside.

The hallway was dark and narrow; so was the one at home, but ours contained nothing more than a hallstand and a table for the telephone. This one was full of bicycles, standing two or three deep between the door and the stairs which rose steeply to a darker landing, uncarpeted.

'Mind the bikes,' Pat said, redundantly. We had to sidle round them as they lounged there, pedals outthrust, handlebars akimbo, like a bunch of yobbos blocking the pavement outside Woolworth's. Pat was on her way upstairs and I went after her, risking one glance over the decaying banister to see what lay below, and then wished I hadn't. A doorway with no door stood beyond the stairs, and through it I could see a room with no floor. The joists were there but the boards had gone, and the skirting board had gone, the window frame too. Through the space where the glass had been an ubiquitous buddleia leaned in and ivy had its fingers over the sill, ready to climb through.

I leaned unwisely outward to see further, the banisters swayed spongily under my hand and there was a tearing sound as if the whole structure were about to come out by the roots. Accustomed to the dark now I looked back down the stairs. What little sunshine was dribbling in through the ivy-stifled fanlight fell upon the bicycles and I saw that they were skeletons; tyreless, saddleless, wheelless in one case, stripped clean and abandoned. I turned the corner to the landing and found it blocked by an unattached gas stove. Then Pat opened the door somewhere ahead and light spilled out, illuminating a second flight of stairs, little more than a ladder, with no risers, and another door with boards nailed across it.

'Come on,' Pat said, beckoning, and I followed her into the room where the light was coming from.

It was at least a whole room, ceiling, window, floor intact. There was even a carpet, and it was furnished. At first sight it seemed to contain enough furniture for the whole house. By the window was an oak dining table and four chairs with red plush seats; jammed up against it a cretonne-covered settee whose two accomplice chairs stood knee to knee in front of the fireplace. The rest of the space was taken up by a sagging double bed and a kitchen cabinet. Everything was very clean and very old, from the balding candlewick bedspread to the sheepskin hearthrug which, glimpsed between the armchairs, had been worn down to the skin itself in places, leaving small outcrops of fleece upstanding like clumps of pallid moss.

'Shut the door,' Pat said. She took off her school mac and hung it tidily behind the door. There were several other garments clustered there, like overcrowded bats, so I draped my blazer over the bedpost. Pat took our school bags and stacked them in the corner, out of the way. Space was at a premium.

'Do you want some tea?' she asked.

'Yes, please.' We had become very formal and polite, as if we were making conversation in a public place.

'Sit down, then. It won't take long.'

I sat on the sofa. Pat made the tea. In a way, this did not take long because it was calculated to the point of maximum efficiency, given the parameters, as we say now. From a cardboard box in the hearth, she took a sheet of newspaper and a bundle of sticks. Even with my limited knowledge of building materials I recognized lath and split floorboard, although I had learned to recognize them only in the last ten minutes.

'I'm quite warm,' I said. It was early October, very mild, and the room itself, with the window shut, was not only warm but stuffy. Pat took no notice. She crumpled the newspaper into the grate, built a tent of wood over it, set a match to the pyre and sat back on her heels to watch it ignite, now and then adding another stick of wood, strategically positioned. When it was burning well she laid on three lumps of coal, curious compressed things called Betteshanger nuts, and stood up.

'Keep an eye on it, will you?' she said, casually. 'I'm just going to get some water.' From the top of the kitchen cabinet she took down a black iron saucepan, wiped the inside with a teatowel, and went out. For a while I remained where I was, on the sofa, listening to her footsteps on the stairs; then I got up, crossed the room—in three strides—and looked into the cabinet. In the top cupboard was crockery, white, thick stuff, and a jug full of knives and forks. The bottom cupboard contained a flat iron, a dustpan and brush and a shoe box full of cleaning equipment; dusters, polish, Brillo pads, detergent. I closed the doors, listened for Pat returning, and hearing nothing lowered the flap in the middle. That section was the larder. It held a packet of tea, a bowl of sugar, a half pound block of margarine, a jar of mixed fruit jam, half of a sliced loaf, the slices curling stiffly, and a bottle of milk. I began to understand. The kitchen cabinet was the kitchen.

There was still no sound of Pat's return. The room possessed one other door, almost obscured by the table and chairs. But there was just enough space to open it, and I did. What lay behind was obviously a cupboard, except that there was a bed in it, a camp bed with rickety crossed legs and covered by a grey army blanket. At that moment I heard a noise on the stairs, pushed the door to and hurled myself down in front of the fire, blowing industriously on it just in time, as Pat came in with the saucepan.

'Oh, thanks,' she said, in that same casual tone. I moved aside and she put the saucepan on the fire, balancing it on the three Betteshanger nuts, as if on a trivet. Then, 'Shall we finish our French while it boils?'

She dug the text book out of her bag and we sat on either end of the sofa, doing our homework. Occasionally Pat looked critically at the fire and added another Betteshanger nut. I kept wondering where the water had come from. It was becoming painfully apparent that this was Pat's home, all of it; this one room and the adjoining cupboard. Was there a bathroom? I wanted to go to the lavatory but dare not ask, for fear of what I should find.

After about half an hour the saucepan, which had no lid, began to steam. Pat arose and lowered the flap of the kitchen cabinet, laying out milk jug, tea pot, cups, saucers, and surreptitiously sniffing the milk bottle.

'Do you take sugar?'

'One spoonful, please.' We might have been duchesses, so painfully correct were we. Pat measured one spoonful into each cup and one spoonful of tea into the pot. A faint agitation was discernible round the sides of the saucepan. My mother's insistence of a warm pot and boiling water came to mind, but it was already getting on for five o'clock. If we wasted any of that precious water warming the pot, if we waited for it to come to the boil, I might have to leave before tea was served, as Pat was well aware. The saucepan had barely begun to hiss before she emptied it into the teapot, which she stood in the hearth, in the hope of catching any extra heat that was going.

We took our tea to the table, perched uncomfortably on the red plush seats of the dining chairs. A plate of biscuits had appeared, the kind called Rich Tea, which always left me wondering what Plain Tea could be like. There were four. We took one each, tacitly acknowledging that to have more than that would constitute a serious breach of etiquette.

'I've got some biscuits in my room,' Pat had said, dodging into the cupboard. She did not know I knew it was a cupboard. I did not say, 'Oh, can I see your room?'

'Have you lived here long?' I asked, beginning to comprehend why my mother and her acquaintances communicated in such idiotic platitudes. It was not that they had nothing to say to each other, but there was so much that they could not, dare not say.

'About two years,' Pat said, stirring her tea. I'd had first go of the spoon. Now that Pat had it she hung on to it, waving it about like a lorgnette to lend social poise to the conversation. When talk flagged she stirred her tea, vigorously. It had to last. Our two cups had emptied the pot; the pot had emptied the saucepan.

'Do you know, I live just round the corner, in Livingstone Drive, and this is only the second time I've been up here.'

'Up where?'

'The Crescent. I came up here once on my bike.'

'There's a marvellous view up here,' Pat said. 'At the front,' she added.

She was too late. In my hurried prying while she was out of the room, I had not got around to looking out of the window. Now I leaned back and twitched the curtain aside to see what lay behind The Crescent, and immediately regretted it. At the back of the houses lay a fan of rubble-strewn gardens, collapsed brick walls, corrugated iron sheeting, elder, fireweed, wild hops and the ever-present buddleia. At the end of each garden was a small brick shed with, and in some cases without, a slate roof. The one at the end of Pat's garden had its roof and showed some signs of use, for there was a path beaten to it through the long grass and fireweed. Now I thought I knew where the lavatory was.

'We'll be moving soon,' Pat said.

'Will you? Where?'

'Back to London, probably. Mummy doesn't really like it down here.'

'Down here', I imagined, meant the Medway Towns, as opposed to 'up here' which was The Crescent. Born and bred in the Medway Towns I felt a stir of protective indignation. What right had anyone to find fault with 'down here', particularly someone who lived 'up here'?

'Why did you come, then?' I asked, tactlessly.

'Oh, Daddy's work, you know.' She looked me squarely in the eyes and tapped her knuckles with the tea spoon, daring me to commit another solecism by asking what, exactly, Daddy's work was. I had already been giving fast and furious thought to the problem of what to tell my mother when I got home. She would be full of questions about the household; she always was, trying to fit new acquaintances into the complex structure of her social fabric. When we turned the corner at the top of

Wellesley Road I had thought all would be well. I could tell my mother that Pat Coleman lived in The Crescent and our friendship would be encouraged. It had crossed my mind, after seeing the area, that it might be prudent to gloss over which particular house Pat lived in ('I didn't notice the number, honestly, Mummy . . .') but one look at those back gardens made me realize that it wouldn't matter which house I named, it would be all the same. The whole of Rockingham Crescent was the same, and I knew what my mother would call it; a slum.

Here at the rear of the house, out of reach of the sunshine, the room was growing dim. A pale square floated above the fireplace, the lowering sun reflected off a pane of glass somewhere out in that wilderness at the back. The fire glowed dull and smoky.

'Shall we put the light on?' I asked, without thinking.

'Oh, no,' Pat said, quickly. 'It's nice sitting here in the firelight.' She seemed to speak of cosy winter evenings, logs, roaring flames, thick curtains drawn against the dark; not this dingy indoor twilight and the smouldering Betteshanger nuts. It was still light outside, and it was silent.

I lived in a terraced house. Not that we had noisy neighbours but you knew there were people on either side, next door but one, further up the road. There were voices, shouts, radios playing, cars starting up, dustbins clashing. Here in The Crescent it was silent, the only sound the occasional sighing of the fire, a creak as the coal shifted. Admittedly we were high above the town, but even so . . . not a dog barked.

At last we had to admit that we had finished our tea.

'I'll just clear all this up before Mummy gets back,' Pat said.

Where was Mummy? 'Shall I help?' I said.

'Oh, no.' She gave a little laugh. 'It won't take a minute.'

She put the milk and biscuits into the cabinet, stacked the cups and saucers and teapot on to the breadboard and went out of the room. I stayed at the table, half inclined to follow and see where she did the washing up, half relieved that I wasn't going to have to find out. But it was a malicious impulse that made me get up, cross the room and press the light switch. There was a bulb with a fringed shade hanging at one end of the room, but it did not light up. There was a table lamp on the mantelpiece, plugged in at the wall. I pressed that switch too. Pat enjoyed sitting in the twilight because the electricity was turned off; and so was the gas, no doubt. The disconnected stove was on the landing. I opened the door and stood outside, by the stove, listening. From far away, down below, I caught the clatter of crockery and became aware of a vibrant hissing that seemed to rattle the bones of the house. Pat was washing up in cold water, straight from the main. Had that involved certain judicious adjustments to the stopcock in the street? When I heard her footsteps returning I dodged back inside again and was back at the table when she came in.

'What time did you say you had to be home?' she asked, stacking the cups and saucers into the top of the cabinet.

'Six-thirty.'

'It must be nearly that now.'

It felt as if I had been there for several hours, but we

both knew it was no later than five-forty. A bedside clock with a domineering tick stood on the window sill.

'Yes. I'd better be going.' I looked round for my bag and at the same time we both jumped. A door had slammed downstairs. I had jumped because I was long past expecting to hear any evidence of life, but Pat looked seriously alarmed. There were footsteps on the stairs.

I was shrugging on my raincoat and did not notice, at first, till I looked up and saw her holding out my bag, eyes staring, mouth open, hopelessly urgent. Hopelessly, because the footsteps were now dragging along the landing. The door opened and a woman came in, and behind her a child, a little boy of about five. The boy looked tired, the woman looked exhausted, beyond mere tiredness. She wore a headscarf, scuffed suede boots and, in between, an ugly gingery coat with bristles rather than a nap. I had seen her before. I recognized the coat. I had seen her a dozen times, walking down Stanley Street, waiting in the Post Office, queuing in the fish shop; and I had seen her before a thousand times. She was every refugee, in every newsreel, in every war film, dressed in the only clothes she owned, all character erased from her face by the same blow that had smashed all hope, all resilience.

She looked at me and that beaten face did not alter in any degree, but from somewhere she found a voice.

'Why, Patsy, is this a school friend?'

And she turned to me, holding out a claw that my grandmother would have disowned. I suppose she was thirty-five at most. 'How do you do?'

If my mother had heard her on the telephone she

would have reported, 'Very well-spoken.' She was well-spoken, like Pat, a quiet respectable voice with no particular accent.

I took the claw and shook it. 'How do you do?' I said, as I would have said it to anyone. 'I'm sorry I've got to go. My mother's expecting me.'

'Yes, it is getting dark,' said Mrs Coleman. It was certainly getting dark in the room and Stygian on the landing.

'I'll see you on Monday,' Pat said, as she always did on Friday evenings.

'Yes. Don't come down. I'll see myself out.'

The door closed behind me and immediately Pat's mother said to Pat, 'Oh, how could you? How *could* you?'

'She's my friend,' Pat said, woodenly. I was manoeuvring round the gas stove at the time.

'But to bring anyone to *this* place . . .'

I was on the stairs.

'Doesn't look as if there'll ever be any other place,' Pat said, without rancour.

'You lit the fire!' The voice was anguished now. 'Oh Christ, that's the last of the coal.'

I was in such a hurry to get away I almost forgot my bicycle parked in the area and had to go back for it. That slowed me down. In any case, I was in no hurry to go home; I had a story to concoct, after all, so I wheeled the bike along The Crescent, looking up at the houses as I went. And now I saw. The Crescent was derelict, every window boarded up, paint peeling, stucco crumbling, the areas choked with refuse. From the corner of Stanley Street at the top of the hill, where I had first seen them, I looked back and saw again the Hanging Gardens of Babylon, just as I had on that summer afternoon three years ago.

'You're early,' my mother said. 'Anything wrong?'

'I've got a lot of homework,' I said.

'Did you have a nice time?'

'Yes. Huge tea.' I was so hungry I felt sick.

'Is it a nice house?' How loaded is that word nice.

'Lovely. Right at the top of the hill. I came back along Rockingham Crescent. Doesn't anyone live there now?'

'No one's lived there for a couple of years,' my mother said. 'It's condemned. A shame, really. They must have been lovely houses once.'

Condemned. That word has made me fell ill ever since. I should never have gone back. The Hanging Gardens must have been near their end that first time I set eyes on them. I never went there again. Pat and I were not *that* friendly, not afterwards, and that was none of my doing although I was relieved by her coolness subsequently. I wouldn't have understood how to proceed, knowing what I knew, but she didn't seem to expect it.

'They moved,' I said, when my mother proposed a return visit. 'They were just about to move when I went there. All their stuff was packed.' It was several years before I learned to admire Patricia Coleman, even if she had used me as an accessory, for exercising her right to ask a friend home to tea, like anyone else.

4

A Can of Worms

The desk, where the cash register stood, was probably the most valuable item in the shop, although wear and tear must be reducing its value daily. Every time the drawer of the cash register shot out the desk legs jarred and a furtive click indicated that the left-hand cupboard had opened underneath.

Dora picked up the routine quickly, her fingers that had initially faltered over the keys skipping more surely with each transaction; price of each book, sub-total, cash tendered, total—the drawer opens, the cupboard opens, put in money, take out change, slam drawer, slam door. It would become an automatic sequence very soon, Dora guessed, when trade picked up and she had to serve one customer after another. At two o'clock, only half an hour since she began, people were still filtering in one at a time, and not all of them bought books.

'When does it start getting busy?' Dora said. Lou, the supervisor, looked down from her stepladder.

'Some days it doesn't,' she said. 'We aren't exactly W H Smith, are we?'

'It looks quite crowded, sometimes,' Dora said.

'It doesn't take much to make a place this size look crowded.' Lou climbed down the ladder, balancing gracefully with both arms full of books. As she set foot on the floor a little cloud of dust rose from the books and haloed her fluffy hair in the sunshine. 'I shouldn't wear white too often, if I were you. Nothing collects dust like books.'

Dora glanced down at her T-shirt.

'It's an old one.'

'Sure,' Lou said, 'but it doesn't look too good if you go on the till after you've been in the basement. We have coffee at three and then change places. Jo—she's downstairs, sorting stock—will come up here, and I'll take you down and show you what she's been doing. Tomorrow you might be sorting first—that's the *really* dirty work.'

'Shall I be doing that next?'

'No, I think I'll put you on shelving for now, looking round, seeing where the different categories are, finding gaps, bringing up replacements from downstairs. That way you learn where everything goes. We try to make sure that the shelves never look empty. People think we're running out of stock, which we aren't. You've seen what it's like in the basement.'

The basement was the first thing Dora had seen when she dropped into the FreshWater bookshop and offered her services during the holidays. She passed it regularly, always looking in but never entering until today when she saw the poster in the window; *Volunteers wanted: can you help us?* When Mum had sent her out to find a job neither of them had considered voluntary help in a charity bookshop, but smarting from two rejections at supermarkets—'It's the eczema, dear'—Dora had decided that what she needed to feel at that moment was *wanted* and she began to feel wanted when she was directed to the basement and saw the voracious gleam in Lou's eye.

'Can you do Saturdays?' was the first thing Lou had said, even before she had climbed out from among the wobbling stacks of books, but then she had hesitated when she saw the scarlet patches on Dora's wrists. 'Eczema? Won't the dust be a problem?'

'It doesn't weep,' Dora had said.

'Well, you won't be down here all the time,' Lou said, to Dora's relief. The low-ceilinged basement housed a cupboard with *Kitchen* on the door, a cupboard with *Cloakroom* on the door, and several thousand books.

At three o'clock Jo, who turned out to be an elderly-auntie type, came up to take over the cash register and Dora went below again. Lou was in the kitchen cupboard with a jug kettle and coffee jar; as Dora came through, Lou's arm snaked out in a dextrous manoeuvre and placed a steaming mug in her hand.

'How's it going?'

'Fine,' Dora said. It was fine, sitting in the sunny window, watching people pass in the street, pause and look in at the display. One thing she'd learned very quickly was not to catch the eye of potential customers. She had smiled at some and they were the ones who smiled back, shifted their eyes and then passed by, feeling pressured.

The window display was made up of either very ancient books that looked as if they might be valuable ('If they were they wouldn't be here,' Lou said) or very new ones with bright jackets. Down in the basement the new ones could be seen in all their minority, here and there among the ancients like the salad filling in a wholemeal sandwich.

'Do you sell all of them in the end?' Dora asked as they drank their coffee.

'Good Lord, no,' Lou said. 'They get three months on the shelves—look, they all have a date on the fly-leaf. If they haven't shifted by the sell-by date we reduce the price and put them in the bargain bookcase. The real no-hopers go for pulping—in there.' She kicked a large cardboard box. 'Even that brings in a bob or two, mainly hardback fiction. Nobody seems to want that; they prefer paperbacks. You probably noticed, we keep a big rack of those by the door. Lures 'em in.'

A young man with a beard skittered down the stairs and shimmied between the dingy stalagmites of books without dislodging any of them, like a blind man showing off in the dark.

'You'll have the whole lot down one day,' Lou said, unimpressed. 'Tony, this is Dora, joined us today. Tony does our pricing.'

'I'm the realist,' Tony said. 'No one ever made money overestimating the public's generosity.' He smiled at Dora and turned right, into a dark cul-de-sac beside the cloakroom, shucking off his jacket as he went. Then the light came on and Dora saw what he would be pricing. Like the rest of the basement that corner was lined, floor to ceiling, with shelves, but the floor was stacked with more cardboard boxes. 'That's the new stock,' Lou said. 'Tony sorts and dates it and decides the price.'

'What did he mean about overestimating the public's generosity?' Dora said. On the evidence of the basement alone, the public seemed to be overwhelmingly generous about donating books.

'You'd be surprised how many people try to beat you down over the price,' Lou said. 'Everybody thinks books are expensive, however little they cost. And they nick them.'

'From *here*?'

'Oh sure. If you look in that cupboard under the desk you'll find a list of our regulars; the ones to look out for. And you'd be surprised how many of these are nicked in the first place. Schools, libraries . . . people seem to have a moral gap when it comes to books.'

'A *book* shop?' Mum said, when she went home that evening.

'A charity bookshop,' Dora said, resolved to let the worst be known from the outset. 'It's voluntary. I don't get paid.'

'I know what voluntary means,' Mum said. 'I thought the whole purpose of this operation was to earn some money.'

'That was your idea,' Dora muttered. 'I just wanted something to do.'

'Very laudable, but I did suppose that remuneration would come into it somewhere.'

'There wasn't anything,' Dora said. 'I tried three shops and they all wanted somebody permanent. I *won't* work in a burger joint—'

'Vegetarianism's turning out quite an expensive indulgence, isn't it?'

'Yes, well, we can afford it, can't we?' Dora said, sourly. 'I don't blow my allowance in six weeks like John does. Anyway, I don't think they'd have me. The supermarkets wouldn't, not even for shelf-filling.' She held out her blotchy hands. 'Anyway, wouldn't you rather I was doing something really worthwhile than nothing at all? It's not for ever; only till September.'

'Every day?' Mum sighed.

'Every afternoon,' Dora said. 'One-thirty till five.'

'So perhaps you can find something that *pays* for the mornings?'

'I'll go on the game, if you like!' Dora said, slamming out of the room.

Gran was in the hall, tweaking a jar of delphiniums into shape. Dora would not have been so base as to assume that she was eavesdropping, but Gran, in her flimsy gold-stitched mules, was clearly neither going out of the house nor coming in, and the flower arranging looked suspiciously like a piece of stage business when someone has missed a cue.

'I suppose you heard that,' Dora said, gracelessly.

'I still have my hearing and my teeth, thank the good Lord,' said Gran, slipping into her old crone routine. It was hard to imagine anyone less like an old crone. At seventy-five Gran did not make the tactical and tactless error of supposing that she and Mum might be taken for sisters, but if she had claimed to be sixty no one would have doubted it. Her face was lined, but her immaculate blow wave was still more blonde than white, and her figure elegant rather than angular, her movements agile.

'Spry, dear,' Gran said, when anyone remarked on this. 'Not agile, not at my age. Old ladies are spry.'

She gave the delphiniums an appraising look, over the bridge of her patrician nose, and turned to Dora. 'I think I could carry off a coat that colour, this autumn,' she said.

'What colour?'

'Delphinium blue. I could have my hair rinsed to match.'

'Oh give it a rest, Gran.'

'Claws in, darling. Whatever the row's about, I've no part in it.'

'She thinks I ought to be earning for the good of my soul. What's the point of giving me an allowance and then expecting me to go out and earn more? I don't *need* more.'

'Rosemary believes in the dignity of labour,' Gran said, vaguely. 'The Protestant Work Ethic, whatever that is.'

'We're atheists.'

'Yes, but *Protestant* atheists.'

'I *am* working,' Dora said. 'Not getting paid for it doesn't make it less like work. I suppose the real reason is that I'll enjoy it. As far as Mum's concerned, work isn't work unless it makes you miserable.'

'She's not really in a position to know, is she?' Gran said, with silky malice.

'This is really worthwhile,' Dora said. 'It's for charity, a Third World self-help project; sinking wells.'

'You're going to sink wells, darling? How arduous.'

'No, of course I'm not,' Dora snapped.

'I didn't hear as much as you seem to think,' Gran said. 'Come upstairs and tell me *all*.'

Gran had her own sitting room on the first floor, what would have been the most desirable bedroom, with a little iron balcony overlooking the street. She had furnished it herself, restfully, in white and shades of blue. If she did dress to match the delphiniums she would merge with the upholstery, like a moth on a tree trunk.

'It's a second-hand book shop,' Dora said, 'down

Lower Dukes Lane, between Culpepper's and the craft gallery.'

'I thought that was the Trattoria Bologna?'

'It used to be. They've only been there a few months. It's the FreshWater Trust, the charity is, you know, like Oxfam and Help the Aged, only they just sell books and prints, only Lou says they don't get given many prints.'

'And who is Lou?'

'She's the woman who runs it. All the staff are volunteers but she says they're always short-handed in the summer holidays. She's got this poster up in the window, asking for helpers. She almost *fell* on me when I said I could do Saturdays.'

'And this is just Saturdays?'

'No, every afternoon. If Mum's really worried about the money I'll go and wash up at the Duke's Head in the mornings,' Dora said. 'But I don't see why she should be. She can't pretend she thinks I should be earning my keep. She's always having to bail John out.'

'I'll have a word,' Gran said, superbly, indicating that a word from her was all that was needed. 'Now let's have a gin and tonic to celebrate.'

'Celebrate what?'

'Oh, I don't know . . . any excuse. We can drink to charity, fresh water, self-help—no, I'll make them. You're much too free with the tonic.'

Dora watched Gran, still supple, stoop without effort to take out the glasses and bottles from her little sideboard that stood on the same bow legs as the desk in the shop. Gran was not at all free with the tonic, the main reason why Dora had been about to mix the drinks herself. Mum fretted discreetly about Gran's gin, and begged Dora not to encourage her, as if Dora smuggled it into the house after dark. Dora saw no reason why Gran should not get roaring drunk if she felt like it. If you couldn't do as you pleased at seventy-five, when could you let rip? You might as well die at thirty, a prospect that appealed increasingly to Dora. What was there left, after that?

Lower Dukes Lane sloped steeply from the modern shopping centre to the narrower streets of what remained of the mediaeval city round the cathedral. On Saturday afternoon Dora, who had been buying shoes, approached it from the upper end and stood for a moment, under her umbrella, gazing down towards FreshWater Books. The lane turned slightly to the right just there, and she could see into the shop for in the dull, rainy afternoon, Lou had switched on the lights, illuminating the shelves, the racks, the desk where she would herself be sitting shortly. At the moment the place was occupied by a woman in a red blouse, not Jo—Jo was fatter than that—and Lou had brown hair. Dora had a sudden vision of herself sitting at the desk, seen from a distance, seen by someone else standing under an umbrella in the rain and thinking, I *must* go in there.

She ran down the lane, which was paved but wide enough to admit delivery vans, closed the umbrella and entered the shop. There were several damp customers standing about on the green carpet tiles, but Lou, on a stepladder as usual, saw her at once and climbed down.

'You're early.'

'Does it matter?'

'No, it's perfect. Susan—' she waved to the woman in

red '—has got to go, and Paul's just rung to say he won't be in. Can you take over on the till for now? I know I said I'd put you on to shelving but, well, Saturdays are like that.' She laughed apologetically.

'That's all right. I like it on the till.'

'Most people think it's terribly boring.'

'I can always look out of the window.'

She took Susan's place at the desk and watched her, huddled into a white trench coat, hurry up Lower Dukes Lane, pause at the top where Dora had paused, and plunge away to the left, heading no doubt for the car park.

'Excuse me . . .'

Dora turned guiltily and saw a man standing at the desk, holding a pile of paperbacks.

'Holiday reading,' he said. 'Have you got a carrier bag?'

Dora nodded, smiled efficiently, madly trying to remember the sequence of keys on the cash register, getting it right but taken unawares when the desk door swung open and hit her knees.

'You get used to it,' Lou said, stretching past her to prop up an open book with enticing colour plates, in the window display. 'Actually, while it's open, you might as well read what's inside. I'm not sure that it does much good, but we can't just ignore it.'

Dora stooped below the level of the desk and saw that taped to the inside of the cupboard door was a number of file cards, written out in different hands.

Short, middle-aged man. 'City gent' clothes. Middle Eastern? Carries briefcase. Always pays for purchases but needs watching.

Elderly woman, tall, well dressed. Wears a grey cape. Never buys anything.

Tall youngish man, 'down and out' appearance. Usually comes in about 4.15 and stays till closing time.

Teenage girl, dyed blonde hair, black jeans. DM boots. Has a friend with her, always a different friend. Friend usually buys something. A team?

'Our regulars,' Lou said. 'We've got the mirror, of course, but there aren't enough of us to keep watch all the time. The person who usually does spot something is on the till and you can't leave that to chase them up the road.'

There was a list of regulations taped to the wall above the desk. The first one, in large type, read, NEVER LEAVE THE TILL!

'I mean,' Lou said, 'until they're out of the shop they technically haven't stolen anything, and by the time they're outside and you've called someone off the shelves or rung down to the basement, it's too late. Don't worry about it,' she said, 'but if you should recognize one of our chums, let us know. Don't feel you've got to stare at the mirror the whole time. It's as much a deterrent as anything.'

All the same, Dora found herself paying rather closer attention to the convex mirror that hung in an angle at the back of the shop. With the lights on it was more obvious than it had been yesterday, but too distant to show more than the kind of view seen from the wrong end of a telescope; incredibly detailed but miniaturized beyond mortal eyesight.

At five to three another stranger came up from the basement, a young woman in dungarees. 'Aline,' she introduced herself. 'You must be Dora. It's your coffee break—oh, hang on, I've got something for you. Nothing exciting, I'm afraid.' She held out a badge identical to the one that she and Lou and the others wore, a white disc printed in blue with the word FRESH-WATER and, inevitably, three wavy lines underneath.

'One of us,' Aline said, affably; Dora pinned it on her sweater and went downstairs to Lou and coffee in the basement, one of them.

'You've had a good day, I can tell,' Gran said, when Dora came in, shaking water from her hair, having left the umbrella in the basement during a fugitive bright period at closing time.

Gran was drinking sherry in the kitchen while Mum washed salad at the sink, presumably keeping an eye on her intake.

'Can I have one?' Dora seized the bottle before Mum could refuse. Instead she frowned, only half playful.

'I don't know . . . the boozing gene skipped a generation with me.'

'What about your Martinis? Anyway, I don't booze, I just feel happy. Isn't that the best time to drink?'

'Certainly more sensible than flying to the bottle for consolation when you're miserable,' Gran said, and slyly raised her glass in Dora's direction, meanwhile nodding towards Mum. She had had her word.

Dora sat and watched them bickering companionably while the rain rattled on the window panes, shaking the green leaves in the garden, and almost longed for winter, the three of them shut in warmly against the world.

'What are you smiling about?' Mum said.

'I've had such a nice day. I do like the shop.'

'I've been looking out some books for you to take in on Monday,' Gran said. 'Good stuff, too, none of your Victorian three volume novels and bound sets of Punch.'

'Of course not,' Dora said. Gran's books were all upstairs in her rooms, in glass-fronted bookcases, and in beautiful condition.

'No first editions,' Gran said, 'but they might fetch a pound or two for the cause.'

'They aren't suffragettes, Mother,' Mum said.

'Well, all good works are a cause, aren't they?' Gran said, expansively. 'Just another drop, darling, while you've got the bottle.'

'Sorry, Gran, there isn't another drop.'

'You're joking.' Mum's head jerked round.

'No.' Dora upended the bottle and shook it. 'Don't look at me. I've only got about half an inch here.'

'Don't worry,' Gran soothed them. 'I've got plenty upstairs.'

Mum had turned back to the sink, shoulders slumping. 'I'm sure you have.'

Dora was half-way down the steps on Monday before Gran overtook her.

'Can't wait to get there, can you?' Gran complained.

'No,' Dora said, frankly. In her mind she was already striding down Lower Dukes Lane.

'What about the books?'

'Books?'

With a beautifully assumed look of mute reproach Gran held out a dark green carrier bag.

'Harrods! When do you ever go to Harrods?'

'When I'm passing,' Gran said, loftily.

'I bet you only went once and kept the bag to flash around. Maggie, at school, bought a blouse in a jumble sale with a Harrods label, and when it got too small she cut off the label and sewed it into a coat from C&A.'

'Vulgar ostentation.'

'And this isn't?' Dora looked inside and saw seven pristine dust jackets. 'Gran! These are new.'

'Not at all. Just *cared for*. You know I can't bear to see lovely things mistreated.'

'You'd better not come to the shop, then. We've got some horrid old tomes in the basement. I suppose you want the bag back?'

'Well . . . it's a perfectly good bag.'

'You *do* flash it around, don't you? All right, I'll bring it back tonight.'

At the corner she turned and looked back. Gran was standing on the steps, posed like a svelte model in a magazine, framed by the tendrils of wisteria that grew over the porch. This year's fashions for the *Older Woman*, Dora thought. What an old ham she is; and walked on, her mind half in the shop, half back at the house with Gran and Mum, except that Mum was out at work. How had elegant posy Gran produced blunt, dour, downright Mum? And how had Mum in turn produced extravagant John, and Dora who knew so well how to be happy? Obviously Dad and Grandpa had contributed something. Grandpa had been a chartered accountant, not the most fanciful of professions, and Dad's capacity for being happy had removed him from the scene six months after Dora's birth, in search of fresh wife and children new.

She entered the shop with confidence, the FreshWater

badge in place on her lapel, and went straight to the basement. Lou was telephoning and waved as Dora reached the foot of the stairs.

'New books,' Dora mouthed, holding up the Harrods bag.

Lou, who probably supposed that a passing donor had given them to her on the way in, smiled in the distracted manner of people on the telephone who can never quite shake off the conviction that the party on the other end of the line can see them, and pointed towards the hole in the wall where Tony did his sorting and pricing.

Tony was currently manning the cash register. Dora had no idea what kind of a system he operated, for the boxes of books seemed to have been opened at random, in no particular order, but near the entrance was an avalanching heap of carrier bags awaiting their turn. She would have deposited Gran's contribution on top of the pile, but if it indulged Gran's harmless vanity to bring back the Harrods bag it would be no harm to take out the books and leave them in a more prominent position on one of the boxes. In any case, she thought, looking at the mould-spotted volumes in the box through which Tony was apparently working, it would surely lift his heart to see Gran's gifts, shining cleanly in the murk. She folded the bag, shoved it in her pocket, hung her jacket next to Lou's raincoat and sprinted up the stairs.

'You'll never guess what I've just sold,' Tony said, as she relieved him at the till. 'Remember that frightful anatomy book I showed you on Saturday?'

'The one with a spider living in the spine?'

'That one. A South African tourist came in a little while ago and *grabbed* it. Said his grandfather owned one and he used to spend hours looking at the pictures when he was a little boy. What sort of a boyhood was that? I asked myself. I thought it would be a cert for the pulping box,' Tony said. 'Are you taking over?'

'Yes please.'

'You *like* being on the till? Don't you get bored?'

'That's what Lou said. No, I do like it. I enjoy watching people.'

She changed places with Tony and watched him, descending from the sunlit shop to the dismal regions below. Tony, she had learned from Lou, was a teacher, generously giving up his holiday to help out, as well as coming regularly on Saturdays. Why didn't they have teachers like him at her school? instead of the glum functional types who seemed to regard the students as some kind of industrial raw material; rather than people, and often asked her irritably what she had to be so cheerful about.

Tony was at work around the corner when it was Dora's turn to go down for coffee, but as she was boiling the kettle she heard his voice:

'Good Lord, this is one or ours.'

'What is?' Lou said.

'Balcon's *Flora of Northern Europe*. I thought I recognized it.'

'I suppose someone's decided not to keep it after all.' Lou sounded preoccupied.

'I remember putting in on display. Look, here we are, on the fly-leaf; June. That must have been the first week I was pricing, at half term. That's my writing.'

'Maybe it was an unwanted present.'

'Well, whoever bought it only had it for six weeks. It could take six months to get through this thing. How odd.'

Dora stirred her coffee. She was fairly sure that the *Flora of Northern Europe* was one of the books in Gran's carrier bag. Holding the mug gingerly for fear of spilling hot liquid on delicate volumes, she sidled out of the kitchen cupboard and peered round the corner. Tony and Lou were standing with their backs to her but she could see that Tony had already begun pricing the books from the Harrods bag. One lay open with his yellow pencil laid across it.

'How much did it go for last time?'

'Ten pounds, it was in perfect nick. It still is. I'll just change the date and put it out again—for the same price. It doesn't look as if it's been opened.'

'There's a gap in the window display,' Lou said. 'Dora! Oh—there you are. When you go up again just check the window display, will you? I noticed some wide open spaces.'

'You can put this in for a start,' Tony said. He leaned across the boxes and handed Dora the *Flora*. 'It's a bargain, though no doubt someone will try to haggle over it.'

Dora took it as Tony bent again over his open book and picked up his pencil, murmuring, 'I don't suppose this one . . . no, Dillons.'

Dora sat on the stool that held open the kitchen door and balanced the *Flora* on her knee while she leafed through it. Definitely it was one of Gran's. As soon as she saw the spine she recognized it from the glass fronted bookcase in Gran's sitting room, the one between the two long windows. She felt vaguely uneasy; the feeling had first stirred back there in the pricing room when Tony said, 'Whoever bought it only had it for six weeks.' If Gran had bought it only six weeks ago she would surely have remembered something, said something like, 'Oh, that's where I bought Balcon's *Flora of Northern Europe*.' Or, when she gave Dora the Harrods bag this morning, something like, 'This one's going back where it came from. Can't think why I bought it,' or something, *something*.

When Dora saw Lou and Tony looking at it she had been about to say, 'My grandmother sent those'; now she shivered with relief that she had held her tongue, had taken the books out of the Harrods bag that she had so blithely waved at Lou when she arrived, for now she had herself remembered something. When she first came home and told Gran about the shop, Gran had not known where it was. She recalled that distinctly. Gran had known the *place*, all right, but she had thought it was still a restaurant.

Dora rinsed out the coffee mug and went to look on the stock shelves for books to take upstairs. Everything was labelled; Psychology, Engineering, Pets, Fiction, Medicine—some of the medical books were so old they were dangerous; one advocated igniting gunpowder to cauterize dog bites, and the shelf which carried the most inviting looking items was labelled simply, Display. These were the books that could be stood on top of the shelves upstairs, laid on the table by the door or exhibited in the window. It did not seem to matter what they were about, they were in sufficiently good condition to command a decent price. Making a tray of an atlas she loaded it with a dozen or more and set off upstairs. As she went she heard Tony's voice; 'Well I'm damned, here's another; July.'

She did not wait for the rest.

Mum was in the little back garden, tenderly drawing tap-rooted weeds out of the borders. Dora stood watching her for a few minutes, marvelling at her patience. Dora always tugged too hard and left half of the root behind to sprout again. Gran never weeded at all, but floated about with a trug over her arm, snipping off dead heads with the languorous motions of a dying ballerina. Only Mum really enjoyed gardening, the continuous day to day dedication to flowers and weeds alike; planting, pruning, mowing, mulching, digging. She was humming under her breath, something enjoyably mournful in a minor key. She never did that in the house.

I never want to leave here, Dora thought. I'd like us to go on for ever, Mum in the garden, Gran upstairs and me coming home from work. I want to be me coming home from work *always*.

'Mum?'

'I thought I heard you come in. Had a good day?'

Mum, I do love you even if you are an old crab and won't let Gran have her gin. 'Of course I did.'

'Remember to get the eggs?'

'They were out of free range. I'll go down to Assad's later, if you like. Where's Gran?'

'Having an *aperitif*, I expect.' Mum's voice dulled again. 'Don't leave it too late, will you?'

'He's open till ten.'

'You know I like us to eat by eight.'

'I'll go in a minute,' Dora said, turning back to the house. Why did they have to eat by eight—in case Gran had too many *aperitifs*?

Gran was standing on the balcony with a long-stemmed glass in her hand.

'Flirting with the rain,' Gran said.

'Is it raining?'

'A few drops. I'm daring it to do its worst.' She trilled her fingers along the wisteria fronds. 'Do you want some Rudesheimer?'

'I'll wait till dinner. Mum's doing a soufflé, only I've got to go out again for the eggs.'

'Don't rain on my Dora,' said Gran to the sky.

'Gran, where did those books come from?'

'Books?'

'The ones you gave me for the shop—oh, here's your precious bag. Gran, they were almost new.'

'Then they should fetch a good price.'

'They will.' Ten pounds for Balcon's *Flora*. 'But didn't you want them? You can't have had them long.' June. July.

'Good heavens, darling, I buy on impulse, you know me. Sometimes I make the most ghastly mistakes, that appalling linen dress for instance. I've never worn it. I'm even worse when it comes to books. "I *must* have that," I think. "Just the thing for long winter evenings," but,' she shrugged sweetly, 'when the long winter evenings come, I've utterly lost interest.'

'You really should come along to FreshWater,' Dora said, blushing. 'It's a much cheaper way of buying on impulse. We've got some lovely bargains.'

'I dare say I shall, darling. Where did you say it was?'

★

'Just us today,' Lou said on Wednesday. 'Jo's rung in to say she's got some kind of bug. Tony's had to take his son to an athletics meeting, though I should think they'd be rained off at this rate.'

'Till or shelving?' Dora said briskly. Susan was already half-way up Lower Dukes Lane, her umbrella tugging wilfully in the wind.

'If you're happy at the till . . .' Lou said, smiling, as if she could scarcely believe it, and rushed to the basement where the phone was ringing.

The shop was empty. Dora sat at the cash register and craned her neck to inspect the window display. There were four books at least which looked brand new. She had identified Balcon's *Flora of Northern Europe*, in its central position, from the top of the lane.

Outside, the rain fell steadily; a mill race gurgled in the gutter that ran down the centre of the pavement. Up and down, with dogged tread and resigned expression, trudged inadequately clad tourists, and bareheaded macho blokes in sodden T-shirts who didn't care, trekking between the building site at the bottom and the Duke's Head at the top, but when the downpour eased and the sky lightened, people once more paused to look in at the window, and after a while began to venture inside.

Lou ran up and down with fresh stock for the shelves. A German in a plastic mac bought the *Flora* and Lou instantly darted in with a replacement, the complete works of Jane Austen. On the same trip she deposited, on the trolley near the door, a big glossy coffee-table book, *An Illustrated History of the English Theatre*. It was so large that Dora, seated at the till, could see the jacket design quite clearly. Predictably, a painting of The Globe with, especially predictably, Shakespeare standing on the stage, as if Shakespeare were the only person in England who had ever written a play.

It was while she was staring at the book that she noticed activity in the convex mirror that hung at the back of the shop. It took a moment to work out which set of shelves it reflected; the Natural History section, out of her line of sight, behind the stair well, but she recognized the figure at once, even though it seemed no larger than Shakespeare at The Globe. What she did not recognize was the grey macintosh cape. Dora leaned down and opened the door beneath the desk. It stuck a little and she had to jerk it, evidently it normally responded only to the drawer of the cash register. Squinnying sideways and attempting to watch the mirror at the same time, she read the second notice from the top, that was taped inside the cupboard door.

Elderly woman, tall, well dressed. Wears a grey cape. Never buys anything.

Dora saved time and motion by serving a customer before bothering to close the door; now trying to divide her attention between his Anglo-French queries about street maps, and the figure in the mirror which was, in fact, no longer in the mirror but proceeding round towards the Fiction corner, magisterial in its exquisitely tailored cloak of dove grey cloth, a little spotted with rain about the shoulders.

Dora shut the drawer and the door. The Frenchman left with a cheery wave. The grey cloak was moving towards the display table where it paused. Scrutinized, head bent. Straightened up and shrugged regretfully;

no, nothing, absolutely nothing, nothing at all. And left.

Dora saw at once that Shakespeare had left as well and spun round to look out of the window where the grey cloak was unhurriedly adjusting itself, as well it might, to conceal what lay beneath. Dora broke her rule about catching the eye of passers-by—this was hardly a passer-by—and looked, and looked.

Gran looked back, smiled and nodded and walked away down Lower Dukes Lane in the cloak that Dora had not known she owned. It was a friendly look, candid, impersonal, and held not a hint of guilt, or duplicity, or recognition.

5

Crocodile Time

Two weeks at Christmas when it's absolutely empty, and three in September when it *seems* empty because all the foreign-language students have gone home and the University isn't up, but the rest of the year it's wall-to-wall rubbernecks. It starts about Easter, little bunches of people silting up at Carfax and wandering down the High Street staring upwards at an angle of forty-five degrees (what are they staring *at*?) but as spring turns to summer the little bunches gradually become bigger bunches and they stop wandering and start shuffling, and sometimes there's a great mob with identical day-glo back-packs and the shuffling turns to marching and Carfax looks like the Last Night of the Proms and suddenly it's Crocodile Time.

I've heard that it's worse in York, but I don't believe it. Nothing could be worse than Oxford when the crocodiles come out.

It isn't only the numbers, it's what they do. Cameras are OK. People with cameras just stand in the middle of the road on traffic islands and take long shots of the colleges, or else teeter on the edge of the pavement and photograph relatives posing in front of Laura Ashley, glaring at you if you get in the way. But at least with a snapshot you can get *out* of the way. The real buggers are the video freaks, the ones who take moving pictures of

Magdalen Tower and the Sheldonian Theatre, as if buildings look more real when they are in motion, if you see what I mean. Look, folks, an action shot of the all-singing, all-dancing Martyrs' Memorial.

I don't know how many home videos I've featured in as a walking extra, restless native, and so on; not always walking, either. For example, one hot day last year George and I spent the morning in Angel Meadow with a few cans and a funny ciggy that some kind soul had given George, and then we went into town and did our Pratman routine, George in a balaclava and wearing swimming slips over his tracksuit bottoms. Pratman has, of course, special powers, but he's taken this vow never to use them because his metabolism is based on anti-matter, so his daring deeds consist of leaping out of doorways, flexing his biceps and saying, in what George thinks is a New York accent, 'Hey there, little girl, can I be of any assistance?'

For obvious legal reasons he rarely says this to real little girls. Instead he tries it on grown women, grown men, bus drivers, vicars and, on this occasion, tourists. It went down with varying degrees of success. Some of them laughed, some of them—the British ones—thought it must be Rag Week and gave him money (we made £1.23), some took one look at the balaclava, assumed he was the IRA and screamed, and some of them turned the video camera in his direction.

I don't play a very important role in the Pratman adventures, being Neville the Boy Psychopath, in fact I don't do *anything* (which is just as well) except rush up to George crying, 'Gee, Pratman, wuddawedo *now*?' and gallop away again with my cloak rippling in the wind at speeds of up to four miles an hour. Countless home videos taken in Oxford last summer must feature George in his green knickers, jumping out of doorways, and me whizzing past yelling, 'Gee, Pratman, wuddawedo *now*?'

You can imagine it; living rooms in Chicago, Frankfurt, Tokyo, Bangkok: 'And here we have a peaceful afternoon in Oxford, England. Observe, please, the merry English going about their daily lives in quaint national costume.' Enter George, leaping out of the Body Shop, biceps a-twinkle. 'Hey there, little girl, can I be of any assistance?' Enter me. 'Gee, Pratman, wuddawedo *now*?'

Sometimes we molest the crocodiles—this is when we *aren't* being Pratman and Neville the Boy Psychopath. The best way to molest a crocodile is to join it. There is a number of ways of doing this. If we are feeling fit we trek down to Oxpens and catch it as it gets off the coach, but this never lasts long because the minders are doing headcounts and can usually speak good English, like the time we were mingling with a croc of German kids and up comes this very lovely big lady in tiny shorts and says 'What do you want?' in an unencouraging sort of way. 'Oh, we want to practise our German,' says George, leering at the shorts.

'How unfortunate,' says Fraulein X. 'We are Martians, now sod off.' Usually their English isn't *that* good.

Better crocodile sport is to wait till they really get into their stride, on that wide bit of pavement in New Street alongside Nuffield College, and then infiltrate, which is easy because all you have to do is walk slowly and let them engulf you from the rear. Then, like the Fifth Column, you begin to promote alarm and despondency from the inside. This works best with English-speaking peoples (we aren't total xenophobes).

'Pity about the Bodleian,' says George. 'I mean, fancy pulling it down just to build an Asda. I think that's really bad.'

Or, 'Have you seen the hurricane damage at Christchurch?'

Or, 'I wonder if the nuclear accelerator building's still sealed off.' I think myself that that last one is pure genius.

We are not, in fact, xenophobes at all, but if you've got two intelligent young lads with an urge to commit a nuisance (and who hasn't?), the intelligent thing to do is to make use of the local raw material which in our case is tourists. This is not to suggest that the nuisance is necessarily directed at the tourists; sometimes they just come in useful, as in the case of the Guided Crocodile.

The Guided Crocodile doesn't get out of a coach, it assembles on corners around the city and is made up of singletons and renegades from official crocodiles. People put out crocodile bait in the form of notice boards: 'See Historic Oxford with friendly undergraduates': 'Tour of Historic Oxford conducted by cheerful graduates' (marvellous what a degree can do to your attitude): 'Walking tour of Historic Oxford with experienced guides'. They lurk, these notice boards, at strategic points around the city, some with little clocks on them; next tour starts at 10.30 or 11.15 or whenever.

'Why don't we do that?' George said one day, as a crocodile with thirty-six beautiful legs set off for Christchurch behind a friendly undergraduate.

'What, join a crocodile? Gee, Pratman—'

'No, you drongo, lead one. Quite apart from the

money we might meet some interesting people.' He was looking at the legs.

'Where would we take them?'

'Where everybody else takes them. Broad Street, Sheldonian, Bodleian, Radcliffe Square—'

'Quite,' I said, 'and that's as far as we'd get. These cheerful guys can take them round the colleges, that's what they want to see. We couldn't do that, we'd never get past the gate.'

'What about Guided Riverside Walks?'

'How can you charge people to walk along the Thames?'

'Easy, you start at Folly Bridge and walk all the way down to Iffley Lock, and then they'll need you to find their way back again.'

'They'll just turn round and walk upstream, won't they?'

'Not if we make historic Iffley Road part of the tour.'

'What about Cowley? Take them to see the Austin Rover plant—if it's still there.'

'The iron foundry—'

'The railway sidings—'

'The Ice Rink—'

'The Polytechnic—'

'Alernative Oxford! The parts other tours cannot reach.'

We were, by this time, sitting on the grass by the canal basin (very alternative) being mugged by ducks who are a depraved mob down there and will stop at nothing for bread.

'Wild-life tours?'

We were running out of ideas.

'Why don't people want to see alternative Oxford? How do we know they don't?'

'Because alternative Oxford looks just like anywhere else. It looks like all the bits of London they saw from the coach, or Birmingham, or Wigan—'

'Let's put up a sign at Oxpens: *Oxford full: try Wigan instead.*'

It was getting chilly down by the water so we wandered back into the city to find a Guided Crocodile to harass.

You need a straight face and a good memory for this one, also a lot of bottle. To begin with we made it up as we went along, but we soon realized that to be completely convincing we'd have to formalize it, abide by a few rules; dammit, we needed a grammar.

What we do, see, is ask questions in a foreign language. Between us we have three foreign languages and one of them is Latin. Unfortunately the guides nearly always speak French or German, and Latin has contributed words to so many other languages that everybody recognizes it. And ying-tong noises don't work, either, because they sound exactly that—ying-tong noises. It was George who pointed out that the reason foreign languages, English included, no doubt, sound like gibberish the first time you hear them, is because you can't tell where the words end. The most you can hope to identify is a sentence; individual words come later. So Crocodile-speak is made up of sentences, delivered very fast, with a few key words chucked in when we wish to communicate with the natives. But we were agreed on one vital thing: *we* had to know what we were saying.

We need a pretty big crocodile, too, or the guide

rumbles at once that we were not there when the tour left base. This time we found a huge one, winding round the Radcliffe Camera, one of our favourite places, for reasons which will become apparent.

'*Olvé*,' says George. '*Decuercut bastis, ikut*?'

'*Parkut*,' says I. (All verbs end in 'ut'; it makes life simpler.) '*Decuer ab mala, e mala baskis mir devardut, zu*?'

Which, being translated, means, 'Oh my goodness, whatever is this great big round building with a dome on the top?'

To which I am replying, 'I cannot imagine, but it is certainly very large and can't possibly be a telephone box, can it?'

'*Devardut ni, devardut nu*,' says George. ('Well, it might be, but there again, it might not.') At which moment we close in on the guide, smile hopefully and point.

'*Gdansk?*'

Gdansk is one of the key words and means, as you have no doubt deduced, 'What is this?'

The guide, being no slouch at foreign lingo, cottons on immediately.

'This is the Radcliffe Camera,' he says, slowly and rather loudly. 'This—is—the—Radcliffe—Camera.'

George and I look at each other in consternation.

'*Camerask devardut*?'

'*Oh, vehen decuer mala, mala, mala ignut deber, zu?*' and George whips out his Instamatic.

We look at it, we look at the Radcliffe, we look at the guide and smile kindly.

'*Giversut! Baskis djang, seher*.' ('Pull the other one, it's got bells on.')

If you've never been to Oxford—is there *anyone* out

there who hasn't been to Oxford?—you may not know that the Radcliffe Camera is not for taking photographs with, it is a library, and if you happen to know Latin then you may be aware that *camera* means chamber, which the Radcliffe is, inside; one big room; but how could two innocent East Frodoxians be expected to know that? We come from East Frodox, me and George, as we try to explain if anyone tries to ask.

'*Oriesis Frodoska mihirgut,*' we cry, with our arms flung in the direction of the rising sun (and East Oxford, incidentally). '*Zemianos modrovi mala, bar gamel zermut, revier sevenfourseven zuti, saskut Ithro dodona.*'

('We travelled many, many days on a camel and then boarded a great silver bird which brought us to a beautiful place called Heathrow.')

Then we spot a rather handsome edifice opposite the Radcliffe and as one man turn on the guide.

'*Gdansk?*'

There is, of course, a limit to how long we can keep this up, and we have to be careful that we don't nobble the same guide twice. Once we landed ourselves with a guy who must have been a linguistics expert because he kept trying us with different languages, and we had a hell of a job getting away.

But on this day, (oh yes, there was a day, a day of days) I was alone. It was the end of August, the crocodiles were getting thin and scarce and hardly worth the bother of molesting. School was due to start in six days' time, even for me and George, in the Sixth Form. One is expected to show up, at least on the first morning, and although we don't have to wear school uniform in the Sixth we are supposed to look a bit respectable, in case there are any new parents knocking about, probably, and it was a good excuse to invest in a new pair of trousers.

There was the usual dispute about this.

'*More* clothes?'

'I'm paying for them.' I have this evening job in a deli up Cowley Road.

'The fact that you can afford them doesn't mean that you have to buy them,' etc., etc.

Most of my wages had gone on this really nice leather jacket I got in a sale, and I thought it was worth going back to the same shop to see if they had anything left in the final reductions. I'd just got off the bus in Cornmarket and was crossing the road to the shop, when I saw her, on the corner of Market Street, with a map.

It was the way she was standing that caught my eye. Oxford, after all, is full of people with maps, littered with them; great big maps and little street guides and limp photocopied things. It's odd, really, because you can practically see from one end of the city to the other; the part that the crocodiles infest is about the size of Trafalgar Square, and who needs a map to get round that?

But there she was, in this very slim yellow sun dress that was slipping off one shoulder, and a tote bag made of old prayer mats over the other, holding her map. She had no shoes on, I think that's why I noticed her, that and the way her hair, yellow hair, really yellow, almost the same colour as her frock, fell over her face when she bent her head, so that I could see the back of her neck with the sun glinting on all the little gold hairs there. She *was* golden, all over.

I changed direction.

When George and I are in a socially responsible mood we assist people with maps, and even when we aren't we never knowingly misdirect anyone, not even crocodiles, although the temptation to send them off up Cowley Road is often strong. Coming to the assistance of people with maps is a good way of getting to know them. Sometimes we offer to take them where they want to go, and sometimes we stick around when they've got there, but this applies only to lady singletons; we do not stick around with crocodiles.

This was exactly in my mind when I saw my golden girl in Market Street, but as I swerved, some dickhead in a car—which is prohibited, Cornmarket being pedestrianized; that is why it is full of buses—came belting down on the left and almost rubbed me out. We had a full and frank exchange of opinions and he revved off again, straight towards a cop, I was pleased to note, and when I reached the pavement she was gone, my girl, but with that colouring she showed up at a distance. She was on her way up Market Street, actually passing the covered market as it happened, and heading for Turl. Trousers be damned; I followed her.

When she got to Turl she didn't, as I'd hoped, pause and consult the map again (thus giving Neville the Boy Psychopath a chance to rush up and cry 'Hey there, little girl, can I be of any assistance?'); she strode—yes, folks, no shoes, you see—she *strode* straight across, down Brasenose Lane, the silky yellow skirt trilling round her legs and the silky yellow hair rippling in the breeze like the aforementioned cloak of Neville the Boy Etcetera. Which last thought made me very happy that I was alone and not accompanied by George, particularly not accompanied by George in his Pratman outfit. George does not appreciate the finer things and parts of our city are very fine indeed. He would have appreciated my girl, but he would have seen only the girl. He wouldn't have realized that to truly appreciate her, you would also have to appreciate Brasenose Lane.

I knew just how she was feeling, having come out of Cornmarket, which is your average British shopping area, along Market Street, which is straight grot, and then finding herself in Brasenose Lane on a summer morning. The lane was in shadow and at the end of it the sun was shining in Radcliffe Square, on the big oval of grass where the Camera stands, on the walls of All Souls, on the cobble stones of Catte Street. And when she reached the end of the lane the sun hit her and she seemed to ignite, glow, she burst into flames, I mean, the air *shone* round her.

I felt my heart lift, I really did, I shed pounds, I was weightless, like being on the moon. I was bounding along Brasenose Lane in ten-metre strides. I took off. She turned right.

I wasn't so far behind her now, but I hadn't been trying to catch up, I was enjoying the view so much. Impure thoughts, such as those secreted by George's depraved brain-substitute, had left me entirely. I felt so bright and clean—but I didn't want to lose her. I'm not the kind who can *survive* on beautiful memories, so I accelerated into Radcliffe Square and turned the corner.

There she was, shimmering away down past Brasenose College and into the little alley past St Mary's Church. And there she stopped. I thought she was going for the map again and really stepped on it now, before some other Good Samaritan elbowed in with offers of assistance and evil intentions, but there was no sign of the map. As I throttled back for the final approach she put her hand into the prayer mat and drew out a purse. She handed someone some money; there were several people standing around; and when I arrived I discovered *what* they were standing around; a notice board. I'd seen it all before; cheerful graduates, friendly undergraduates, the next tour starts at 11.30 . . .

She was joining a crocodile.

How could you? I asked her, silently. Do you realize how this wounds me to the heart? I thought you were a free spirit, a lone operator. You are not the stuff that crocodiles are made of.

On the other hand, I thought, I shall know exactly where you are for the next hour and three-quarters. I can follow at a respectful distance.

It was a very scrawny crocodile, average for the time of year, only about two dozen legs; not the kind that George and I would consider interfering with. Then I noticed the guy who was taking the money. He was looking at my girl in a mildly carnivorous way, and tour guides are not like doctors. They don't, I imagine, get struck off for unprofessional conduct with the crocodiles, and this specimen looked as if he might get very unprofessional. There was only one thing for it. I withdrew three quid of my trouser money and went up to him. Reader, I did it. *I* joined a crocodile. Oh, the shame of it.

Now George and I had never been in at the start of a tour and we didn't know how it worked, so it hadn't occurred to me that the guy who takes the money isn't necessarily the guy who leads the crocodile, so I was not best pleased—not in the least pleased—when who should come trotting up the High Street but Magdalen Mike.

We call him Magdalen Mike because in spite of his being a cheerful graduate or whatever, we once heard him do a really chilly put-down on a nice little Indian lady who had asked if the tour included Magdalen College?

'In Oxford,' said our man, 'it is pronounced *Maudlin.*'

'No,' said the little lady, who clearly hadn't understood a word. 'Please, we see Magdalen?'

'Maudlin,' he said. '*Maudlin.*'

'Magdalen?'

'MAUDLIN!'

Which is why we have ever since called him Mag-da-len Mike. It was probably Mike who started us on the East Frodox kick in the first place, him or someone like him, so you can see why the sight of him caused a frost upon my soul, especially when I guessed that he was heading for my crocodile. We had met before.

I looked at the ground. I don't have a particularly memorable face, but I do have a memorable language problem and I could see that I might have trouble losing myself among the massed ranks of this crocodile, because massed they weren't. But I had just parted with three quid's worth of trouser, as it were, and I wanted my girl who was standing not two metres away, soaking up the sunshine and converting it to twenty million volts, just like our nuclear accelerator.

'Why do we wait, please?' said a crocoperson, after the money man and Magdalen Mike had conferred for a bit and half past eleven had long gone but no one else had gone anywhere.

'We are waiting for a party to join us, sir,' said Magdalen Mike with a terrible smile, brought on by the effort of saying 'sir', and I screwed my eye up-side-ways and looked where Magdalen Mike was looking and, oh God, here came the rest of the crocodile, another sixty legs at least, swarming over the pelican crossing from the bank where they'd been clogging up the queues changing travellers' cheques. I've been on the butt-end of those queues many a time.

But to look at it another way (you can see what an optimist I am) these were definitely the massed ranks in which I could lose myself. Moreover, they were all talking a language which sounded very much like East Frodoxian. Now that Magdalen Mike's attention was diverted elsewhere I could make my move. The existing members of the croc were getting ready to go, shouldering bags and swinging cameras into position. My own little Van den Graf generator pushed her hair out of her eyes, adjusted her prayer mat and stood—alone! I sidled round a hefty Hanimex and there I was where I longed to be, and she turned and smiled, all shining and happy and innocent. Oh, I *was* glad George wasn't there.

We moved off, like a good crocodile, behind Magdalen Mike, down the High Street. Behind his back I took the opportunity to scrape my hair forward into a kind of fringe, which *ruined* the image, man, but changed my appearance dramatically. And I hadn't been wearing the leather jacket last time we'd gone Gdansking. I was biding my time, waiting for a really auspicious moment to open the conversation and praying that she would understand a little English at least, even if she didn't speak it, or alternatively that she spoke the kind of language in which remarks like 'I think you are fabulously beautiful, will you come and have a drink with me?' sound much as they do in English, can be readily translated and answered with a nod. What I was trading on, though, was the knowledge that most people speak English as well as the English do, if not better.

I was half hoping that she'd say something first, such as, 'Oh, I feel faint. May I lean on you?'

But Magdalen Mike had led us safely to the gate of All Souls and it was just as we were passing through it that I felt a really heavy presence beside me, an unwelcome certainty that something horrible was approaching, like that depression over Iceland that's always heading our way.

And a voice in my earhole said:

'*Davar vasien mihirgut, inula libertik mala, zu?*'

This is what we always say when we enter the gate of All Souls, and means, 'Doesn't this remind you of the entrance to the collective farm back home?' The way George was saying it now definitely meant, 'Fancy meeting you here.'

I stole a quick glance at Golden Girl, but she was staring up at the gateway.

'Bog off,' I said, out of the corner of my mouth. George beamed and clapped me on the shoulder.

'*Oh, vehen Bogoff.*' This is not part of the script. '*Oriesis Frodoska mihirgut.*'

'All Souls College,' intoned Magdalen Mike, 'was founded in 1437 by Henry Chichele, Archbishop of Canterbury.'

'*Olvé,*' says George, getting into his stride, '*decuer zin*

Chichele dur Chichele jarut modrovi gamel men Oriesis Frodoska pan dihedin, zu?'

('Ah, now, can this be the Chichele who is the Chichele that introduced the camel into East Frodox at the end of the fifteenth century?')

'I'm not playing,' I hissed, but too late. Magdalen Mike had broken off his discourse on Henry Chichele to look in our direction, a long look that passed through three distinct stages; irritation at being interrupted, vague suspicion and deep dislike. I was waiting for the fourth stage, recognition, but George wasn't bothered. He had no idea why I was there. He certainly had no idea that I had actually paid hard cash to join a crocodile and assumed that while out shopping for trousers I had been smitten with an irresistible urge to annoy one, instantly rushing, with deranged fervour, in the direction of the nearest croc.

'I beg your pardon?' said Magdalen Mike, with a barely suppressed sneer. I was fairly sure that we had only once before interfered with one of his crocodiles, and I knew that he hadn't so far remembered *me*, but George was another matter. I would never mention this to his face because George is as vain as the next man, me for instance, but George looks as if he died last week. His skin is the colour of a peeled banana and you would swear that through his pallid veins courses not blood but embalming fluid. If he didn't wear the balaclava while doing the Pratman act people might be impaired for life and go away convinced that Oxford is the home of the Living Dead.

I could see that Magdalen Mike was fairly sure that he had come across George before and was trying to work out where, but George was bashing on regardless, embarking upon our most ambitious spiel, to the effect that the University of East Frodox is much larger than that of Oxford, but suffers in comparison by being built entirely of two-storey prefabricated units manufactured in Bulgaria out of reprocessed fish boxes; it goes on for ages. I began to shuffle away from George, but everyone had seen him greet me like a dear old mate, and to tell the truth, only Magdalen Mike seemed to be getting the slightest whiff of rat. The rest of the crocodile, it appeared to me, were listening with approval to this courageous character who refused even to *try* and speak English to the English.

Why don't *we* just yell at them in Serbo-Croat? you could see them thinking, and now that I had distanced myself from George I could understand why. He really did sound as if he was saying something, he was so passionate and committed, remembering the dear old Uni back home, all those millions of Bulgarian fish boxes. Then he saw that I was getting away and grabbed my sleeve, urgently.

'*Shmeher!*' he pleaded. '*Shmeher mir devardut nu!*'

This normally translates into something along the lines of, 'Blimey that's a big one, isn't it?' but from the vicious squint in his eye I could tell that today it meant, 'Don't drop me in it, you little bastard, what the hell are you playing at?'

'I think we had better move on,' said Magdalen Mike, evidently deciding that an attempt at conversation with George was a distinct no-no.

George's hand fastened like a manic crab round my leather sleeve.

'*Vehen!*' he cried, waving at Magdalen Mike. '*My vriend—vill—dranslade!*'

Dilemma: did I forfeit my lifelong friendship with George by denying all knowledge of him, or did I abandon any chance of making headway with my golden girl by throwing in my lot with the East Frodoxians? Golden Girl was just standing there, twiddling her prayer mat and looking from me, to George, to Magdalen Mike.

'I don't think there's much point in that,' M M said, with some degree of truth.

'*Scharr*,' I said, nodding vigorously, *scharr* being another key word meaning, variously, 'How right you are', 'fair enough', or 'don't let's argue about that right now'.

'*Med svarga parkut*,' George persisted. He was getting out of hand, now, making it up as he went along. The crocodile was becoming restless. Magdalen Mike turned his back and began heading across the quadrangle.

'Oh, wait!'

They all stopped. Crocodiles are like that, programmed to instant obedience. All heads turned, including Magdalen Mike's, to see who had spoken. It was my girl. She was English. Of course she was English, she was embarrassed; nobody else would have been. She was embarrassed for us, two poor foreigners being browbeaten by an unfeeling Brit.

'I'm sure I can help,' she said, and something about the way she said it made my blood run cold and no doubt had the same effect on George's formalin. She would not be amused when she knew the truth. She was as good and sweet and kind as she looked, and she was *earnest*. She had absolutely no sense of humour. There was no future in it, I saw in an instant. We could go on codding Magdalen Mike all the way round Oxford, but it would mean codding her, too. I looked at her tenderly, took out my diary which was bound in red leather and could, from a distance, pass as a phrase book, and peered in, thumbing the pages.

'Ah, yez,' I said, relieved, grinding my heel, meanwhile, into George's instep, 'my vriend vant—vot you say—zer gehents.'

'The what?' She was trying so hard to understand. Never, in a million years, would she have a good laugh about this afterwards.

'Zer gehents.' Jeez, how explicit was I going to have to get? I made violent chain-pulling motions. 'Zer vader glozzid.'

'*Scharr,*' George agreed enthusiastically. 'Zer vader glozzid *parkut*.'

'Over there,' said Magdalen Mike, frostily, and led his crocodile away. Golden Girl tagged along behind, blushing a little. Whatever it was she thought George had been asking for, it wasn't the loo.

When we got back to the High Street I shoved George up against the wall and pinned him there with a friendly arm across his throat.

'Right,' I said, 'now I am going to kill you.'

'Whaaa? Why?' George said. I let him breathe—once. 'What have I done?'

'What do you think *I* was doing?' I screamed at him. 'I *paid* to join that crocodile.'

'Paid?' His jaw would have dropped if my arm hadn't been holding it up. 'You paid to join a crocodile? Why?'

'I was following someone,' I growled, and let go of him, noticing that a small feeble crocodile had gathered round to watch. Somebody had a video camera trained on us. ('And here are young tribesmen engaged in a manhood ritual.')

'Oh no,' George said. '*Her?*' He didn't have to elaborate. There was only one her it could have been.

'Satisfied?' I said.

'Go back,' said George. 'You didn't have to come away. You paid.'

'How can I?' I said. 'Now she thinks I'm an East Frodoxian who can't speak more than six words of English. Where would I go from here; old Frodoxian mating calls?'

'Get her address. Send her a letter explaining that you write it better than you speak it,' George urged, but without much conviction. He looked really fed-up and pleasantly guilt-ridden. I didn't kill him, but we kind of lost heart after that. Pratman and Neville the Boy Psychopath have gone to that Great Comic Book in the Sky, and this year the crocodiles are enjoying a close season. We're getting old.

6

Party Wall

There will be four of them; he works this out almost immediately; two girls, two blokes. Last year it was three blokes, so quiet and studious that it was long after Christmas before he caught a glimpse of even one of them, a Sikh, whose head in a purple turban appeared surprisingly over the wall at the back, inquiring after a page of his thesis that had blown out of an open upstairs window. Daniel found the lost paper, stuck down behind a flower pot, and the Sikh extended a lean arm over the wall to take it back.

But the wall is seven feet high. The Sikh student must have been standing on a chair to see over it. There has never been any neighbourly chit-chat over these garden walls. The gardens at this end of the street are scarcely more than yards. The one behind Daniel's house reaches just fifteen feet from the back door and the one beside it, on the end house, is even smaller. Daniel's mother has filled their yard with plants in pots; seasonally, tulips, geraniums, tomatoes, chrysanthemums; permanently, azaleas and dwarf conifers. A vine is on its way up the end wall.

Next door has no such embellishments. The first words that Daniel hears from the incoming tenants this September afternoon, are in a high clear voice that exclaims, 'Christ! It's just like a pigsty.'

'It looks all right to me,' says a second voice; male, north country.

'Oh, you know what I mean,' says the girl, 'all these walls and whitewash. Put some straw down and it would make a lovely pigsty.'

'You should know.' A third voice, a second girl.

'Well, it *is*.' Sulky, flouncy, sweet and shrill; he'll always recognize that voice. He knows what she means, too. In July, when the Sikh and his two fellow students moved out, Daniel balanced on the rim of the urn that holds the bay tree, and hoisted himself up to look over the wall. There is nothing in the yard next door, only the four whitewashed walls, blinding white in the sunshine, and the hot concrete slabs that pave it. He can imagine it, knee-deep in straw, with a contented sow slumped in one corner.

'Oh, Jenny!'

Now the detective work begins; careful listening is essential. Daniel sits in his small back room by the open window, and from the open windows next door the voices begin to identify themselves.

'Wha-at?' Her again, the pigsty girl, she's Jenny.

'Which one do you want, then, which room? I'm easy.'

Are you? thinks Daniel. How easy are you, whatever your name is?

'I want sunshine!'

'Then you'd better have this one at the back.'

Next door to me. He touches the wall.

'It's the smallest, though.'

'I don't care, so long as I get the sun.'

The window opens beside him. She is getting the sun

already. Instantly he leans from his, but only in time to see a slim brown hand withdrawing, palm uppermost, getting the sun.

'Duncan!'

'What?' The voice comes from almost directly below him. Duncan is out in the yard, and out of sight. One of the reasons that the yard next door is so small is that a flat roofed extension is built on to the kitchen. Nothing of the yard can be seen from Daniel's window except the top of the end wall.

'Are you having upstairs front or downstairs front?'

'Downstairs—nearer the bathroom.'

'Ah, these weak masculine bladders . . .'

That is what the extension is, the bathroom. These houses were built in less enlightened times. An extension at the back is the only place for a bathroom unless you convert one of the bedrooms, as Daniel's parents have done. The room he occupies would be the obvious choice, being the smallest, but he begged for the sloping roof, the low window. Lying on his divan he can rest his arms on the window sill and stare out. What a pity there is nothing to stare *at* except for the identical backs of the houses in the next street.

When they first moved in, nearly two years ago, he had imagined striking up friendships through those two adjacent windows, barely three feet apart; that was before he discovered that the house, like half the others in the area, is rented to students.

He doesn't yet know the name of the second girl, who has got the middle bedroom, and the upstairs front is as yet unoccupied, which means that there may be a fourth to come.

'Anna!' Duncan calls, indoors again.
The second girl; Anna.

Because the house is on the corner its front door opens into the street that runs at right angles to his own, although it counts as 98 Lockyer Street and not 1 Hereford Street. Unlike the occupants of Number 94, on the other side, people leave and enter 98 unseen. Only occasionally has Daniel passed the door of Number 98 and observed activity, such as the dignified exit of the Sikh in his gown and white tie, off to some university function. Daniel wondered if he would replace his turban with a mortar board when he arrived, but never knew because he never saw him again although he witnessed the other two moving out, loading audio systems and suitcases into the cars of stunned-looking parents. Then the house stood empty until now.

Next morning, dutifully watering the tubs of late tomato plants, before leaving for school, he hears Jenny call from somewhere inside.

'What time's Russell getting here?'

'Plane's due in at nine,' Anna answers.

'If he's not here by twelve we can leave him a note.'

So, Russell, arriving by air, will be the fourth.

The way to school does not lie down Hereford Street, but a detour is possible. Daniel makes the detour this morning, and coming home again in the afternoon. Hereford Street is long and straight and rises slightly towards the junction, so he can see the porch of the corner house all the way, long before its back windows, and his, come into view. No one enters, no one leaves, but the window of the small back room, next to his own, has been left open. He turns the corner, wheels his bicycle along the side entry, parks it among the flower pots in the yard and goes upstairs to open his window.

The room is stuffy after being closed all day. When he opens the window dazed flies and a wasp, punch drunk from hurling themselves at the panes, rise up from the sill and stagger out. The house is silent. His mother won't be home from work until six, his father till eight. Daniel kicks off his shoes, drops his school jacket and trousers on the floor and falls face down on to the bed, and lies there listening.

From somewhere he hears music—no, *feels* it. The sound is no more than a presence but the beat is solid, pump action music, on and on, like a heart; a heartbeat. It could be coming through the wall but on the other hand it could be coming from the far end of the street. In this warm weather windows are left open all day. Music becomes a shared experience.

He can see the edge of Jenny's open casement. Is she sitting there at her desk; all students have desks, the one in the front room downstairs stands in the bay window. On dark winter mornings he has seen a low light shining behind the curtains. Or is she lying beside him on her bed? Because of the shape of the room and the position of the door, there is only one place to put a bed. Her desk must stand where his does, by the opposite wall.

Jenny, are you there?

A door slams, *their* front door. A voice calls, a man, not Duncan. 'Anyone here?'

No one answers him. Russell has come home to an empty house.

They've left you a note, says Daniel. They thought you'd be here by twelve.

Russell has not found the note.

'Anna? Duncan?' He comes running up the stairs. 'Jenny?' Doors open, boards creak, as Russell runs through the house. Down he goes again, the back door opens and he discovers the pigsty. The loo flushes; he has located the bathroom. Then there is silence. He has found the note. Ten minutes later the front door slams again. Daniel waits for Russell's voice to greet the prodigals' return, but no one speaks. No one has come in, Russell has gone out.

The house is still empty when he cycles down to the running track, but two hours later, as he pedals back up Hereford Street, he sees the whole place lit, the back bedroom window and the middle one, the white well of the back yard, the fan light over the front door. Turning the corner he sees both bay windows illuminated, Duncan's downstairs, Russell's up. Duncan is playing jazz, a big band, but not too loud. Daniel can hear it only because the transom is open. No music comes from Russell's window, but he is in there. Down in the street Daniel sees, through the net curtain, an arm, in a rolled-up sleeve, reach up and shove a suitcase on to the top of a wardrobe.

Down in the yard, putting his bicycle away, he can see Jenny's window, a shadow moving on the wall inside. Anna's window is out of sight, it can be seen only from Hereford Street, but it is Anna's voice he hears, from the kitchen, probably, over a cacophony of jangling utensils, the familiar sound of someone rummaging through a cutlery drawer.

'You'd think there'd be a corkscrew!'

'Have you looked in the sideboard?' Duncan.

'Perhaps they don't want to encourage us to drink.'

'There's a can opener,' Russell chips in. Daniel can't place Russell's accent but he has a carrying voice. He does not raise it—a singer's voice.

'We don't *need* a can opener.' A note of petulance intrudes.

'I'll go next door and borrow one!' Jenny trills, and the shadow vanishes. Daniel is about to rush inside and ransack the kitchen, ready to present her with a corkscrew when she knocks, but Duncan, suddenly in the kitchen too, inquires sarcastically, 'And what's this, hanging up by the egg whisk?'

'That's a corkscrew?'

'What did you think it was?'

'Looks like something used in open heart surgery,' says Russell.

Jenny is in the yard. 'It's wonderfully sheltered out here. Light some candles.'

Upstairs Daniel leaves the lamp switched off and, concealed behind the curtain, looks down. The upper part of the whitewashed walls is alive with a dim, elusive flickering. Glasses clink, a cork is drawn, wine poured; a spattering sound.

'Look out,' says Anna. 'Don't spill it.'

'I'm pouring a libation,' Jenny says. Daniel leans out, careless, enchanted, *listening*.

'I name this house Pooh Corner,' Jenny says, 'and God bless all who sail in her.'

'Why Pooh Corner?'

''cause it's on a corner, and it stinks,' says Jenny's lovely limpid voice.

Perhaps because her room is the furthest away, Anna gradually recedes; by half term, Daniel's half term, she has become a distant echo, indistinct, too distant to be heard clearly, for the weather has turned suddenly cold and all the windows are shut.

Sometimes, cycling up Hereford Street on darkling autumn evenings, he sees the light behind Anna's green curtains; as he turns the corner, Duncan's anglepoise in the lower bay, Russell's in the upper; knows they are there, feels their remoteness. But he feels close to Jenny, so close, lying beside him at night, almost in the same bed. When she draws her curtains he sees her slender shadow on the roof of the extension, hears her opening drawers, closing cupboards. Duncan remains true to his big band sound, Jenny plays any old rubbish, Radio 1, pop tapes, never loudly but he knows because she sings along, always slightly flat, changing octaves dramatically if the notes are too high. One day, from the bottom of Hereford Street he sees, in the yellow haze from the street lamp on the corner, a figure with a bicycle come out of the side gate from the yard and linger, bent over the machine, until he is almost alongside. A man; Russell? Duncan? Before he can see clearly, whichever it is mounts the bicycle and rides away round the corner. He must have been adjusting his rear light, unsuccessfully, for as Daniel reaches the corner he sees the red star extinguished.

In early December there is a warm spell; the windows are open again and a frightful row errupts over the gas bill.

'It's you!' Jenny shrieks. 'You always leave the water running when you wash up.'

'That's because I rinse the plates. You never rinse anything, you just shove it all in the rack straight out of the dirty water and everything tastes of Fairy Liquid.' Anna sounds close to tears. 'What about your baths? Every bloody night—'

Oh, so it's Jenny, is it, every night, every *bloody* night, when he hears water gushing in the extension and heady fumes rise from the boiler vent. Jenny, soft and fragrant in a white towelling robe (how does he know that?) her damp hair wrapped in a towel, singing trite tuneless songs as she prepares for bed. No—she wouldn't go to bed with wet hair—of course! That high unidentified whine that always follows the bath routine; not Russell or Duncan shaving; Jenny drying her hair.

'*Who leaves the gas fire on all night*?'

'Which gas fire? What about—?'

'The gas fire in the living room. I thought we agreed to keep it turned down. What's going to happen when it gets really cold?'

'What about the bedrooms? It's always like a furnace in Russell's room.'

'If you didn't keep the oven heating up for hours, just to cook a pizza—'

'It's an estimate,' Duncan says.

'What?' Everyone says it. Everyone shuts up.

'Look, there, beside the number of units. It says "E". That means it's an estimate.'

'Why've they sent us an estimate?' Anna demands, truculently.

'Because we were out when they came to read the

meter,' Duncan says, with exaggerated patience. 'Haven't you seen a gas bill before?'

Evidently not. It becomes very quiet next door.

Duncan is the first to leave for the vacation. On Saturday Daniel sees a green hatchback drawn up outside the door in Hereford Street, with the hatch up. That evening Duncan's window is dark and his voice is missing from the nightly exchanges. Who will keep the peace now? But they are feeling peaceful, Christmas is coming and Jenny sings *Good Christian Men Rejoice* in her bath. Anna, in the kitchen, harmonizes. Anna has a serviceable voice and stays in tune, inflicting tooth-aching discords with Jenny's bum notes. Then Russell joins in. First Anna, then Jenny, falls silent and Russell's enormous resonant bass fills the house, the yard, the whole street. He loves to sing, Daniel can tell. Otherwise he would have stopped when the girls did.

Good Christian men rejoice,
With heart and soul and voice,
Now ye hear of endless bliss,
Peace, peace, Jesus Christ was born for this,
He hath ope'd the heavenly door
And man is blessed evermore,
Christ was born for this,
Christ was born for this.

'Oh Russell,' Jenny cries, after a very long pause. 'What a *wonderful* voice you've got.'

'Do you sing in a choir?' Anna asks.

Russell does not answer, does not answer audibly, but Daniel imagines him smiling, a little embarrassed at having let himself go, but helplessly pleased at the result.

'Sing again,' Jenny says.

No answer.

'Go on, Russell, sing another one. For us.' She pleads. Does Anna plead too? At last he raises his voice again.

Personant hodie,
Voces puerulae,
Laudantes jucunde . . .

Daniel sees him clearly, this big bloke—he must be big with that voice—standing there in the kitchen singing Christmas carols.

Next day Anna goes too. It's the last day of term for Daniel, Christmas less than a week away. Anna's window is dark, as he cycles up Hereford Street, but Russell's is lit and in the bedroom he can hear Jenny moving about in the next room, packing, perhaps.

'I can't see the point of having central heating if you're going to keep your window open in all weathers,' Daniel's father complains at supper.

'I like fresh air.'

'So do we all, but there are limits. Just leave it open an inch or two at the top, that's quite enough.'

'Why do you always go the long way to school?' his mother asks, while they are washing up. 'It must add about a mile to the journey going down Hereford Street, with that one way system.'

'It makes a change.'

'Not if you do it every day.'

'Well, I'm not late for school, so it doesn't matter.'

Upstairs he opens the window again, which his father must have shut; someone else haunted by gas bills. What difference does it make? It's not as though he turns up the radiator to keep warm. He huddles the duvet round him and leans out.

'Do you fancy going up to the pub?' Russell asks, down in the kitchen.

'Not tonight,' Jenny says. They have the house to themselves. 'I want to get packed and clean up. Then I can go first thing tomorrow.'

'Leave the cleaning,' Russell says. 'I'll do it when you've gone. There isn't much to do.'

'Maybe . . .' Jenny says, doubtfully, and when later the front door slams Jenny is still in her room, singing, opening and closing cupboards. By lunchtime next day she has gone. That night her room is empty and Daniel sleeps alone. For three days more Russell too is alone, his footsteps echoing lonely on the stairs. At night he takes advantage of his solitude to play the music he likes, rather loudly in the upstairs front room. Daniel's mother grudgingly identifies it: Handel's *Messiah*, Bach's *St Matthew Passion*, Fauré's *Requiem* which Daniel learns to love for the heartbreaking violin solo at the end of Side One. Not until the day before Christmas Eve does Russell leave unnoticed, quietly; but that night every window is dark.

'Peace for a few weeks,' says Daniel's mother.

'They aren't noisy,' Daniel protests.

'Not especially,' she concedes,' but you can never tell with students. They break out suddenly . . .'

It is pure winter when they return. Daniel, alone in his room, night after night, opens the window only the prescribed two inches and listens to the muffled gasps of wind gusting over fallen snow. In the yard his mother has dusted the snow off the branches of the potted trees, and he gazes down into a black fretwork of twigs round the blank sheet of the newly covered paving. The whitewash looks yellow.

Soon after midnight he wakes, sure that he heard a door bang. He sits up, listening in the breathless darkness, cold and alert. Somewhere something stirs, creaks; someone is coming upstairs. Silently he pushes back the covers and swings his feet to the floor, but before he can stand upright he hears a door open, a switch click, and outside the window there springs up an eerie illumination, not light, exactly, more a sudden absence of dark. He looks out in time to see, on the white pristine roof of the bathroom, a silhouette that extends its arms and draws the curtains, smothering the radiance. She has come back to him in the night. He lies quite still until he hears her climb into bed, and falls asleep convinced that he can hear her breathing.

Welcome back, Jenny. Oh Jenny, welcome back.

Next evening, pedalling through the slush in Hereford Street, after school, he sees that Anna's window too is lit, and so is Duncan's. He treads carefully up the side entry where his father has put down salt, for the snow has stopped and now it is freezing sullenly. In the yard next door a lid clangs on a dustbin, footsteps crunch, a door thuds shut. All the windows are closed and curtained, the gas vents steam. Daniel cossets his bicycle in an old macintosh, bolts the gate and goes indoors to the kitchen. No one else is home. He lays out his homework on the kitchen table and sits down to it, warmed and solaced by a mug of coffee and the sounds of a meal being prepared next door. The radio plays quietly, no one's voice is raised until they all join in an ironic cheer and the front door slams. Russell has returned at last.

The cold weather persists, windows remain shut, voices muted. Once, from the yard, Daniel hears Jenny's voice, high and plaintive. 'I must have sunshine!'

'Nuclear winter will be like this,' Anna informs her, comfortably, and the door closes.

On the first day of the thaw he *almost* sees Jenny. In his parents' room, looking for a pair of his father's socks to borrow, he hears frantic hammering on the downstairs window next door. Her voice: 'Duncan! Duncan! Somebody!'

But it's Russell's window that opens.

'What the hell—?'

'I forgot my key. I've been ringing and ringing the doorbell. Hurry up!'

'Battery's flat,' Russell says. 'Hang on.'

'Hurry *up*!'

The sleet has turned to rain. She will be standing down there on the meagre concrete border that is all Number 98 can boast by way of a front garden, huddled into a coat, collar up, hair sleeked against her wet, upturned face. He hurries to the window but only in time to hear Russell slam his, and to catch a glimpse of a blue denim leg, a boot, a flying scarf tail switching round the corner.

One day a note comes through the letter box, while they are watching the ten o'clock news. Daniel brings it in and his mother opens it.

'Next door,' she says, passing it to his father. 'Good of them to warn us.'

'Perhaps we can go out that night.'

'What is it?' Daniel asks.

'One of them's having a twenty-first birthday party on Saturday night. She says she hopes they won't disturb us.'

'Suppose they do?'

'Well, we don't hear much from them, do we?'

'Who is it?'

'Who's what?'

'Who's having the party?' Jenny! Twenty-one!

'Does it matter?' His father looks at the note. 'Anna Sampson.'

Of course it matters. He has to know whose birthday he'll be celebrating when he lies there in bed, listening to the music, the laughter, the drinking. Will they dance? Will Jenny dance, will Russell sing, will the party spill out into the pigsty with wine and candlelight?

It's a night of heavy fog. The party remains indoors. Daniel wakes intermittently, aroused by a shriek or a thud, a slammed door, an engine revved in Hereford Street. At three in the morning—he can see by the illuminated numerals on his watch—a voice speaks in his ear.

'Jenny, please, why not?'

He doesn't hear why not, but a door closes, footsteps steal away. Jenny slams the window and draws the curtains.

'Eight weeks. I don't know why they bother. Might as well stay at home and do a correspondence course.' Daniel's mother does not approve of the length, or lack of it, of the university terms, but like it or not, the Easter vacation has begun.

Daniel, still pedalling up and down Hereford Street, with another three weeks of school ahead of him, watches the windows and wonders who will be the first to leave this time. Now that the evenings are light it is harder to work out who is there and who is not, but the weather is warm again; louvres, transoms, sashes, casements stand open, except in Duncan's room. Duncan has made the first move, and next day Jenny leaves, then Russell. This surprises him, he feels put out. Russell is supposed to be last, always last; the last to arrive, the last to leave. But then, he thinks, why stay when Jenny's gone?

How did he know that?

Anna stays. Anna turns out to be a heavy metal fan. Being on the far side of the house her music does not intrude. Daniel notices it only as he cycles down Hereford Street in the mornings, back up in the afternoons, pounding either from Anna's open window or the French doors in the living room below it. At his own window it reaches him obliquely round the corner of Jenny's room or over the roof of the extension. He grows accustomed to it and notices, with something of a shock, hearing it on Good Friday morning, that she is still there; she has not gone home for Easter. Poor Anna, poor shadowy Anna, he thinks, and then realizes with rather more of a shock, that she is not alone. An unfamiliar voice speaks in the pigsty and one day, as he walks down Hereford Street to the pillar box, the door of Number 98 opens and a very handsome man steps out, pausing on the threshold to speak to someone inside.

Daniel stops feeling sorry for poor shadowy Anna.

One morning the green hatchback is at the door again.

Duncan has returned and presumably Anna's man made a tactful departure beforehand, for over the wall comes Duncan's inquiry: 'Is this one of Russell's trainers?'

'Must be,' Anna replies demurely.

'Looks a bit on the small side.' Duncan sounds puzzled.

Who will be next? Daniel wonders and is not surprised, on his way home, the following afternoon, to see Jenny's window open, curtains stirring gently in the breeze.

At some point during the next day, Russell returns.

'No,' he says. 'I take a size eleven.'

'Someone must have chucked it over the wall,' Jenny says, and Anna does not contradict.

On Tuesday, dustbin day, he sees a blue and white shoe perched on top of the black refuse bag left out by the side gate, and Anna's Easter holiday is over.

Jenny is getting all the sun she could wish for. May, after beginning with rain and high winds, turns hot and still, hot enough for June, for July. June, when it comes, is hot enough for August in New York.

From the steep confines of the pigsty one evening, rise rich fumes, smoke, the sound of sizzling. One of them has installed a barbecue.

'Must feel like sitting *in* a barbecue out there,' Daniel's mother remarks, coughing obtrusively as she waters this year's stripling tomato plants. Later she closes the french windows, loudly. Daniel leaves his window open, listening, listening, but they are eating indoors. Jenny comes up to her room early. Daniel hears the window flung open and eases out his head to look. He sees an arm lying along the sill, a thread of cigarette smoke curling away into the twilight, a brief red flush on the white frame as she inhales. He didn't know she smoked.

The other three are washing up.

'Isn't it Jenny's turn?' Duncan asks.

'She said she had a headache,' Anna says. He strains to listen.

'Is that why Russell's looking so peeved?' The other two, then. 'Where's Russell?'

'I said she *said* she had a headache.'

'Ho-ho,' says Duncan.

Daniel, feeling very fly, steals along to his parents' room, where the window is open, and looks across to Russell's room. It is dark, but Russell is in there, alone with his music, Fauré's *Requiem*, the violin solo at the end of the *Sanctus*.

During cricket practice on Friday some sod slashes his rear tyre and he has to walk home, the bicycle limping beside him. It adds another fifteen minutes to *walk* home via Hereford Street, and it's hot. He's tired, but he must have his fix. He hasn't come home the quick way since September, so urgent is his need to see what is happening at Number 98.

From the end of the street he can see that Anna's window is open, and so is Jenny's. She has left something hanging over the sill; a towel? a skirt? As he draws nearer the fabric gleams in the sunshine, hanging straight and heavy and soft against the white stucco. As he draws level with the wall of the pigsty Russell, in the yard, says softly, 'Rapunzel? Rapunzel?'

Daniel looks up again and steps out into the road for a better view.

'Rapunzel!'

It's her hair!

'What's Rapunzel? What are you talking about?'

'You remember the girl in the story.'

'What story?'

'She was imprisoned in a tower and the prince came by and called, "Rapunzel, Rapunzel, let down your hair," and she did, and he climbed up it.'

'More fool her,' says Jenny. He can just see her head propped on a cushion on the window sill. 'I'm drying it, that's all.'

It's like a cascade of dark water. He always imagined she was blonde. Why did he think that?

By seven the sun has moved round from the back of the house. Rapunzel has long ago drawn in her silken ladder, but she is there, in the room beside him. She is not alone.

'I thought you knew,' Russell says. 'I thought you must know.'

'I don't know what I don't want to know,' Jenny says.

A long silence.

'We haven't got much longer,' Russell says.

'You know what we agreed—on the first evening.'

'We hardly knew each other then.'

'We don't know each other now.'

'I've tried. I have *tried*.'

'You'll have to go on trying.'

'What about when we all leave?'

'*I'm* trying to revise. That's all that matters to me at the moment.'

A very long silence.

'And shut the door when you go.'

*

When will they all leave? The Sikh and his friends went at the beginning of July last year. This July begins with thunderstorms, prolonged and violent. Windows remain shut and although voices carry through walls the words are lost in transit. For three nights the voices rise and fall, trapped in the enclosed room. Downstairs at the front Duncan takes to playing his jazz very loudly. Daniel awaits the heavy metal from Anna's window, but one afternoon sees a red Porsche parked at the top of Hereford Street, and Anna's very handsome man carrying boxes out of the side gate.

'Did you notice his feet?' Duncan says in the kitchen that evening. 'Remarkably tiny tootsies. Remember that shoe? I wonder. . .'

'Nothing to do with us,' Jenny says, sharply.

On Saturday morning the voices are raised again in Jenny's room; the rain has passed and the window is open.

'You said Wednesday!' Jenny shouts. 'You definitely said Wednesday.'

'So, I got the date wrong,' Duncan says. *Duncan*?

'But you promised. I can't get away till Tuesday morning.'

'I think you're making a fuss about nothing,' Duncan says. 'You don't think he's going to break in here and take you by force, do you?'

'I don't *want* to be alone here with him.'

'Then go out,' says Duncan, imperturbable to the last.

Duncan leaves on Monday. His windows are closed when Daniel passes. Jenny's window is open but no sound comes out; she must have taken Duncan's advice. Not until midnight does her light come on, after an evening of very slow music from the upper front room. Next day a taxi calls at Daniel's door.

'Round the corner,' says Daniel's father, roused from the six o'clock news.

'Sorry, mate,' the driver says, 'it's confusing, this bit at the end. You think they'd call it Number 1, wouldn't you?' Minutes later he reverses back into Lockyer Street and heads for the station, bearing Jenny away for ever. It is very quiet, up in the front bedroom at Number 98.

But later that evening, very late, as Daniel lies in bed, watching the moon which is almost full, he hears the window open beside him and wakes instantly from his half sleep.

Is she still there after all?

'Oh,' says a voice; not Jenny's, not a woman's voice.

Daniel turns on his front and leans on the window sill, looking out sideways to see what he has so often seen before; an arm laid along the sill beside him, this time a man's arm. He can distinguish that in the light from the enormous moon.

'Oh, Jenny,' Russell says. 'Oh Jesus, oh Christ, oh Jesus Christ, oh Jenny;' and Daniel, who has never before heard a grown man weep, lies listening to Russell cry himself to sleep on his first and only night in Jenny's bed.

7

Resurgam

From a dell of ferns and mosses the stony track led upward among the rocks, overhung here and there with green budding willow branches, past the cavernous mouth of the open tomb. The hillside was starred with little flowers; primroses, violets, squills, even daisies and early speedwell; tiny beads of moisture freckling the petals. But always you looked upward, over the balding rocks to the barren summit where the three crosses stood, stark, sinister, although unoccupied.

'And what's this?' The slender throat of Rowena Randall's brass plant-mister released a jet of vapour among the fronds around the tomb.

'Selaginella—club moss,' Gilly Morton said. 'Charlotte, do you have to grovel just there? It does rather give an impression of abject devotion.'

'Isn't that what it's for?' Charlotte Morton rose from where she had been crouched on knees and elbows, with her chin resting on her forearms which was as close to the ground as she dared to get in the presence of Mummy and the vicar's wife. Alone she would have lain down on her side, one eye at least on ground level. As she stood up, the perspective declined and the lush little Calvary became a pile of breeze blocks piled against the most westerly arch in the north aisle.

'Of course that's what it's for – within limits. You look

as if you ought to be on a prayer mat, facing Mecca.'

'Most of the devotion went into making it, I suspect,' Mrs Randall said. 'It's been here a week and this is the third time I've had to water it. I'd have thought Millie would have been running in and out night and day to see that it was fed and watered.'

'Oh well, Millie's a true artist,' Mrs Morton said, tolerantly. 'It's the *creation* that counts. Once she's finished something she loses interest and goes straight on to the next. It was the same at the Patronal Festival.'

'It's awfully clever, though,' Charlotte said. 'I mean, when you think it's all done with breeze blocks and pâté bowls—and the way she's made the track wind upwards.'

'The hairpin bends, you mean,' Gilly Morton said. 'She got a trifle over-enthusiastic there, I think. It looks like a lay-out for the Jerusalem Grand Prix. Now, are you coming back with me or would you rather walk?'

'I'll walk home,' Charlotte said. 'I just want to stay here for a bit and enjoy the flowers.'

'Well, don't fall into a trance and get locked in,' Rowena said. 'Jeremy will be locking up at six.'

Charlotte, gazing once more at the Easter garden, heard their heels gossip towards the door.

'. . . thinking melancholy thoughts and composing poems about suicide . . .' That was Mummy who had evidently been spying through her desk again.

'Oh well, at that age . . .'

Rowena Randall was a bitch, even if she was the vicar's wife. The heavy door in the south porch closed behind them with a boom and a clatter as the latch dropped. Charlotte kept her eyes on Golgotha, an outcrop of flints balanced on top of the breeze blocks with the crosses anchored in grey Plasticine. Wasn't this the time for melancholy thoughts? these hours between grim Good Friday and the day of Resurrection? There was nothing in the Bible about what they did on that terrible Saturday after the Crucifixion; grieving, shattered, panic-stricken. Sure as hell, though, they hadn't been flower arranging.

Mummy and Mrs Randall had done the altar flowers, two stout brass bowls of rampant white lilies. Lesser members of the flower roster had been charged with the wrought iron stands by the chancel arch, and the odds and sods, as Daddy called them, had been let loose on the window sills where long troughs were vulgarly crammed with loud yellow daffodils and swags of ivy. Millie Gainsborough, architect of the Easter garden, had also been allowed a little fling at the foot of the pulpit, where she had indulged her mania for breeze blocks in a kind of terrace, bearing pots of bulbs. Charlotte, idling in the lane that morning, had seen her unloading the breeze blocks from the back of her Morris Traveller. Millie carried them one in each hand, against her shoulders, her striped poncho flying in the March wind. She looked like Moses, bearing the Ten Commandments on tablets of stone.

The wind had dropped since then. It was chilly in the church now that the sun was descending, but Charlotte knew that she would be stepping out into an unseasonably mild evening. She drew her cold hands up into the sleeves of her jacket and walked the length of the church, from west door to altar, passing from the fresh exuberant scent of the daffodils to the heavy clinging perfume of the lilies in their twin bowls. Tomorrow the silver cross would be released from its protective custody in the vestry safe and displayed between them, flanked by the massive gilt candlesticks that shared its confinement.

'Nothing's sacred, these days,' Rowena Randall complained, after a neighbouring church had been looted of its altar plate, which was why Jeremy would be along to lock up at six.

As she had foreseen, walking out of the chill church was like entering a warm room. Charlotte carefully closed the door behind her, as exhorted by the notice in the porch, in case wayward birds or bats flew in. The notice was tacked up alongside the electoral roll, the flower roster—mainly blank because of Lent—the Bishop's Easter Message and a square of white card ploughed over by Rowena's dashing italic which soared and swooped in exotic pot hooks that tangled themselves illegibly with the line beneath.

HELP!!!! Rowena had exclaimed, winsomely. *Our lovely churchyard is fearfully overgrown. Would any kind souls lend a hand at getting it into shape for Spring? Call me or the vicar on 249. R.R.*

Perhaps it was the proximity of the Bishop's message, but Charlotte envisaged Spring proceeding up the lane in cope and mitre to peer testily over the wall at the tangle of dead grass, ivy and blackberry vines which had rampaged through the churchyard unchecked since the death of Peter Seals, who had husbanded it for fifty years. Even Peter's grave, the most recent and still awaiting its headstone, was engulfed by ground elder and the frayed remains of kecksies and dock.

Somewhere in that wilderness was buried gold, the generous clumps of daffodils that had once gilded the churchyard at Easter. It had been Peter's pride and personal devotion to lay one daffodil on every grave, ancient and modern—and some were very ancient—at dawn on Easter morning, so that when the congregation arrived for Matins it might feel, as Jeremy Randall regularly insisted in his sermon, that every villager past and present had joined together to celebrate the Resurrection. Given that the present population was somewhere around 800 and the congregation rarely more than fifty, it occurred to Charlotte every year that there were certainly more dead celebrants than live ones. This year, though, there would be no daffodils laid out and scarcely any standing daffodils visible, let alone the more discreet clusters of grape hyacinth, primrose and violet. Rowena's girlish plea had been in the porch for three weeks without so much as jogging the elbow of anyone's conscience. Decorating the church, building an Easter garden, were more acceptable services to the Lord than laying in with a scythe to level his acre.

Charlotte stomped on a tussock or two, clearing a patch round the daffodils that stood by the gate. As least they would make a showing. In previous years the whole churchyard would have been clipped in late autumn so that by now the fragrant vernal grass would be showing its little low flowers.

Charlotte sighed and stepped back from the daffodils, straightening up surreptitiously as she heard a car slowing down in the lane. It drew up by the lich-gate and Charlotte recognized the vicarage Volvo. However, it was not the vicar who stepped out, but his son Michael. He looked surprised when he saw Charlotte rise from the herbage on the far side of the gate, but only, she supposed, because he had not been expecting to see anyone at all.

'Oh dear,' he said, 'are you waiting to talk to Daddy?'

Michael Randall was twenty, in his first year at Cambridge. Charlotte was faintly startled to hear him refer to his father as 'Daddy'; it seemed to reduce him by several inches to the little boy in a blue St Thomas's School cap, that was her earliest memory of him.

'No,' Charlotte said. 'I've been helping Mummy with the flowers.'

'Oh, good,' Michael said. He advanced through the squealing gate, another memento of Peter who had oiled it regularly. 'He got called out, so I've come to lock up instead. Have you all finished inside?'

'Yes. Mummy—and your mother—went a little while ago. I was just looking round. It's a bit of a mess, isn't it?'

'Poor old Peter. Who'd think six months could make such a difference?' Michael walked towards the porch. Charlotte walked with him as they seemed to be talking to each other. She supposed this must be what you might call a happy accident, their meeting by chance like this, and she recalled all those times when she had made a detour past the vicarage and he hadn't come out. 'I'd better just look round inside,' Michael said. 'Daddy always does – in case there's someone lurking, I expect.'

'I was the last one out,' Charlotte said.

'I'd better look. Mummy may have left the light on in the vestry. The wiring's a bit dodgy.'

'You wouldn't think a church could catch fire,' Charlotte said, as they went back inside.

'What, all that stone?' The echoing interior was dark now. Michael depressed a switch by the door and a single lamp glowed sullenly in the nave. 'But think of York Minster, how that burned.' He loped up the aisle and into the north transept where the vestry stood. Charlotte waited by the door. She *had* been thinking of York Minster, but not of the stone, only wondering why it was that God allowed his churches to catch fire at all, and especially by striking one with lightning. It seemed so pointless, burning down your own house.

A closing door thudded in the shadows and Michael returned. At the end of the aisle he paused by the Easter garden.

'Isn't it frightful?'

'*Isn't* it?' Charlotte agreed, pulling the plug on her enchantment.

'All those pretty flowers. Do you think Jesus was admiring the violets as he carried the cross up?'

'Do they have violets in Palestine?' Charlotte asked, cautiously. *Why* was it frightful?

'They probably do now. The Israelis seem to grow everything. But really, think of the name; Golgotha; Place of a Skull. If I were making an Easter garden I'd just use rocks—and a few cacti perhaps—and I'd make it look just like a skull, grinning, you know? Gaping eye sockets—the tomb would be one of them. And the only things I'd put on it would be those three crosses at the top and right at the foot, a little tree with a noose hanging from it.'

'For Judas?'

'Exactly,' Michael said. 'I think we should remember him, too. That's what it's all about, after all; betrayal; sacrifice.'

'And resurrection,' Charlotte suggested, and tapped

with her toe the inscription on the tombstone where they were standing, that was set into the floor of the aisle. It was one word only, in curly script: *Resurgam*.

'Well, perhaps on Easter morning I'd let them scatter a few flowers.' He smiled. 'But why does everything have to be so pretty?'

He switched off the lamp and they went out again into the twilight. Charlotte lingered in the archway of the porch while Michael turned the enormous key in the lock.

'Talking of scattering flowers,' he said, 'I suppose no one's going to take over from Peter and do the decent thing?'

'The daffodils?'

'I always thought that was rather a nice gesture. Bit pointless this year, though. No one would see them, the place is so overgrown.'

'Does that matter—that no one sees?'

'Of course not.' She heard, rather than saw, his approving smile. 'I might even get up early tomorrow and do it myself. It would be a nice surprise for Daddy.'

'I'll help.' Charlotte was amazed at her presumption.

'Would you? Well, yes . . . why not? What time does the sun rise? Is there a communion? We wouldn't want to be seen. That would spoil the effect.'

'Sun rise is at six o'clock—about.' Charlotte felt illuminated by a joyous, conspiratorial glow. 'And we had communion here last week. It'll be at Shapton tomorrow.'

'Right, I'll see you here at six. I'll bring some shears or a scythe. We might be able to clear a patch or two. Now, shall I give you a lift home?'

'No thanks, I was going to walk, anyway.' It was hard to say. She would have loved to ride down into the village with him, but why spoil what was to come with anything so prosaic? Better to part here at the lich-gate where they would meet again in twelve hours, at sunrise on a March morning.

She often went for early walks. No one would remark on her absence even if this walk were a little earlier than was customary. The ground would be wet; she put on boots and jeans, regretfully. A frock would have been nicer, but impractical, and she shivered, imagining the discomfort of damp cotton clinging muddily round cold scratched ankles.

As she walked up the lane in the morning half light, which was never quite the same as an evening dusk, she saw that he was there before her, propping his bicycle against the churchyard wall, and at last admitted her secret fear that he might change his mind or forget to turn up.

'Well done,' he said, approvingly, as they went under the lich-gate. 'Now, why don't you pick the daffodils while I do a spot of trimming. How many shall we need?'

'Peter told me last year; two hundred and three. Well, it will be two hundred and six now; Mrs Kellett and John Dawes, and Peter, since then.'

'You'd think there'd be more.'

'That's only the marked ones. There must be a few thousand down there, if you go right back to the beginning.'

'In layers.'

The churchyard, apparently a neat rectangle seen from

the road, sprawled away downhill on the north side, ending in a ragged boundary of ditch and hawthorn hedge. It was here that the daffodils grew thickest, down behind the shed where the bier was kept along with the grindstone on which Peter Seals had sharpened his grave-digging spade. Some of the oldest graves lay on that side, scarcely more than humps in the rank grass. The light was still poor; clouds hung low and there was unlikely to be a sunrise. Charlotte stumbled between the graves, following what remained of the path that for half a century Peter had trodden to and from the shed, and countless sextons for countless years before him; back and forth, digging graves and filling them in, raising mounds, setting stones, unobtrusively clipping, cutting, planting, year in, year out. The practice of placing a daffodil on each grave had been long established when Michael's father became vicar; perhaps it was Peter himself who had begun it.

She could see the daffodils now, not a riotous yellow in the sunless morning but glowing steadily, like shaded candles. She had cut an armful, and laid them in carefully counted bunches of ten, when a sound from the far side of the church made her stand erect and listen. Subconsciously she had been expecting to hear the clash of Michael's shears as he attacked the weeds and brambles on the south side. Now she realized that what she *had* heard was a car, and that what she was currently hearing was a conversation, conducted at a pitch that carried it over the roof of the church and down to where she stood, knee deep in daffodils.

Dropping the bunch that she held, uncounted, she began to run back through the long grass between the graves, to cut round the west end beneath the tower. There was something very familiar about one of those voices—the other, of course, was Michael's—and as she turned by the buttress she saw the roof of Millie Gainsborough's Morris Traveller above the coping of the wall; and there, harassing Michael over the lich-gate, was Millie herself, armed not with a breeze block for once but a sickle. In her leather jerkin and shapeless felt hat she looked like the vanguard of a peasant mob come to strike the first blow against the clergy at the outbreak of revolution.

'Oh!' Millie squawked, when she noticed Charlotte. 'I see.'

Charlotte's disappointment almost took her voice away. 'Have you come to do the daffodils?'

'Considering the state of the churchyard,' Millie said, bitterly, 'it did not occur to me that any one else could *conceivably* have thought of it. If Peter could see it now he'd be turning in his grave.' She pushed open the gate and joined them. 'Did you ask anyone's permission?'

'No,' Charlotte said, and emboldened by Michael's presence added, 'Did *you*?'

'I am on the flower roster,' Millie said, implying that anyone who was not might consider herself lucky to get a mention on Judgement Day. 'And as no one else on the roster seemed to have given a thought to keeping up Peter's life's work, let alone the daffodils—'

She was cut short by the sound of a motor horn, close at hand, and round the bend came Miss Jowett, also of the flower roster, but less of it, weaving up the middle of the road on a bicycle and defying the efforts to overtake of a car that was pursuing her, honking fretfully. Charlotte, still further downcast, recognized the car at once, and the driver.

'Mummy!'

Mrs Morton braked and clambered from the driving seat, and Miss Jowett dismounted, still maintaining her position in the centre of the lane. The basket attached to Miss Jowett's handlebars contained shears, a billhook and a nasty-looking implement with teeth and an adjustable handle. Strapped to the roof rack of the Mortons' Peugeot was a scythe.

'Is this some kind of a conspiracy?' Mummy demanded coldly. 'Good God, Charlotte, what are you doing here?'

'Michael and I thought it would be nice to put out the daffodils, as Peter couldn't do it any more,' Charlotte mumbled.

'It might have been more sensible,' Mrs Morton hissed, 'to have consulted me first. I dare say it seemed very romantic to be frolicking at sunrise in the churchyard—'

'We wanted it to be a surprise,' Michael said, gallantly, but Charlotte, miserable and embarrassed, observed that Mummy's spiteful barb had found its mark. *Romantic.* He was looking at his feet. Why were men always so frightened?

Miss Jowett had leaned her bike insultingly against the nearside wing of the Peugeot and was toying with her implement. It made an unpleasant snickering noise as the teeth ground together.

'It does seem strange that everyone was being so secretive,' Millie Gainsborough sniffed.

'Given the neglect that our churchyard has fallen into

since last September, it hardly seemed worth consulting anyone else.' Miss Jowett gnashed her surrogate fangs. 'Obviously no one cared about maintaining standards.'

'Actually,' Michael said, with a nervous laugh that was very like his father's, 'actually, it seems that quite a lot of people cared. I mean, now that we're all here . . .'

'It would still be a surprise,' Charlotte said, 'wouldn't it?'

'For whom?' Millie snapped.

'For everyone else.'

'*Is* there anyone else?'

It struck Charlotte that in truth no one wanted to give anyone else a nice surprise. The whole thing had been an exercise in self-publicity: Lo! I alone remembered. Except for herself and Michael, of course. Michael really had wanted to please his father and she . . .? She *had* wanted to help, but was that for the vicar's sake, or for the sake of Peter's memory, or was it just for the chance of being alone with Michael at the break of Easter morning?

'You'd better get that thing out of the road,' Millie Gainsborough said to Mummy. 'I can hear a car coming.'

'*Would* you move your machine?' Mummy simpered at Miss Jowett, as she climbed back into the Peugeot.

'I think that Mrs Gainsborough's taking up rather more of the verge than is strictly necessary or safe,' Miss Jowett remarked, to no one in particular.

The car, which they could all hear now, came into view, slowed down and halted, confrontationally, nose to nose with the Peugeot, like two bellicose male beasts contending for the bony carcass of Miss Jowett's bicycle which was now trapped between them.

'Oh Jesus,' Michael said, not at all prayerfully. The latest car was the vicarage Volvo, with Rowena at the wheel, her chin honed for the fray, and behind the car, towed in a trailer, a petrol mower, a rake and, inevitably, a scythe.

'Is something happening that I don't know about?' Rowena asked, glaring out at them through the passenger window.

'A happy accident,' Michael said with a sickly smile, *exactly* like his father's. 'We all had the same idea of coming up here early to tidy things a bit and put out the daffodils.'

Rowena saw him for the first time.

'Oh!' she said. She pronounced it *eau*. 'And what's your part in all this?'

For the second time the Cambridge undergraduate dwindled to a scrawny schoolboy.

'He was here first!' Charlotte cried, wounded with pity for him. 'It was his idea!'

Rowena ignored her and continued to glare at her son who nibbled nervously at the air with his shears.

'I thought it would be a nice surprise for Daddy,' Michael said.

'*Eau!*' Rowena said again. 'And do you honestly suppose that chucking a few *flahrs* about is going to make up for the things you said to him last night, you bigoted little tit?'

'Well, why've *you* come?' Michael demanded. '*You* said that Peter was a sentimental old basket case with his *daffydils*.' Michael was very nearly spitting with disgust. 'You've said it every Easter for the last twelve years! You don't give a damn about the churchyard. You just want to show everybody else up. Well, they beat you to it, didn't they?'

Rowena slammed the gears into reverse and the car shot backwards. The forgotten trailer jack-knifed on its towball and there was much grinding and clashing as the lawn mower bucked in its chains, followed by an evil hissing as air escaped from a wrenched tyre on the trailer. The spectators, who had taken on the appearance of a well-armed garden party, converged on the Volvo to steady and restrain, while Rowena backed it on to the grassy clearing at the end of the churchyard wall.

Charlotte looked hopelessly at Michael. 'I'm sorry.'

'Bit of a fiasco, really,' he said, not returning her look.

'They've ruined it!' Charlotte could have wept. 'Why are people so hateful?'

Michael shrugged. 'Six of us will get done faster than two. I should stay out of it if I were you. Get back to picking daffodils before those harpies beat you to it.'

The flower roster was filing, barging, through the lich-gate which screamed repeatedly as it swung since no one would hold it open for anyone else. When they were assembled on the path they all drew breath to take command.

'Right—' they said, simultaneously.

'Perhaps I could suggest—'

'If I might suggest—'

'May I make a suggestion—'

'If no one else has any suggestions—'

Michael turned wearily to them.

'I've already started,' he said, 'and I might as well go on here along the path. Mummy, why don't you cut round the graves with the mower? Mrs Morton, could you trim the verges? Miss Jowett, you and Mrs Gainsborough could start cutting back the brambles—you've got the tools for it. At least we'll be able to see the daffodils when Charlotte's picked them.'

Charlotte, on her way round the tower again, looked back. Like big sulky schoolgirls the four ladies fanned out to their allotted tasks, cowed by Michael's masculine authority. Since they had no intention of following each other's suggestions, they had no option but to act on his. Anyway, he was a man, even if his mother had just described him as a bigoted little tit, and he had called her a harpy. Charlotte turned and walked on. The sun was rising at last; the light was clean and cool and lay in streaks and splashes across the grassy graves. The daffodils sparkled by the hedge. On the hummock nearest to Charlotte's left foot, unmarked by kerb or stone, lay a long pale bone, underlined by a long dark shadow.

She stopped in mid-stride and looked again. In that arrested second she had had time to assume that what she was seeing was in fact a stick of peeled wood, gleaming in the new young sunlight; but no, it was definitely a bone, a clean white shin, placed accurately in the middle of the grave.

She had no urge to touch it. It did not look like the remains of a meal left by fox or dog; it was a human shin. Nor did it look as though it had worked its way out of the earth, exposed by wind and rain. Her eye travelled to the next grave which was almost entirely overgrown but had a flat slate tablet to mark its place. On the tablet stood a vertebra.

At the same moment someone at the east end of the

churchyard screamed, the scream echoed by Millie Gainsborough's anserine quack, amplified by shock or disgust, and then a little chorus of shrieks and wails. Charlotte spun round and went back, running, seeing as she ran that all about her on the graves that had stood before in shadow and were now illuminated, little patches of white winked cheerfully at her.

On the path by the lich-gate the flower roster was gathered, collectively heaving with outrage. Michael stood placidly among them, holding a rib.

'Black Magic,' Millie was gibbering; 'sacrilege, blasphemy, filthy practices, desecration—'

Rowena clutched at Michael, his bigotry forgotten. 'Thank God Jeremy hasn't seen this.'

'But *when*?' Miss Jowett was bleating. 'When? We were all here . . .'

Mummy turned to Charlotte. 'You were the last to leave last night. Did you see anything?'

'What's happened?' Charlotte said, asking Michael, who was examining the rib with a donnish air and a squint.

'Can't you see?' Millie squealed, and gyrated, arms outflung, as if hooligans were realigning a signpost. 'On the graves—all the graves—'

Charlotte looked, and on each grave – table tomb, headstone or simple mound—lay that same white token; some long, some minute, some curved, some rounded, all shining innocently to greet the morning.

'The police,' Rowena said. 'The police. Somebody call the police.'

'We ought to move them.'

'Not before the police have examined them. Evidence . . .'

'I said,' Mummy broke in, 'didn't you see anything, Charlotte?'

'It was getting dark when we left,' Charlotte said. 'The sun had set.'

'We?' Rowena said, nastily.

'I was here when Michael came to lock up. That's when we decided to come back here this morning, and it was pretty dark then, too. I didn't see anything.'

'This was done by night!' Miss Jowett declaimed.

'How could anyone do it in the dark?' Charlotte said. 'There must be one on every grave; no one could have done it in the dark. Most people couldn't even find the graves by daylight. Only Peter—'

'There are two hundred and six bones in the human body,' Michael said. 'Just enough to go round.'

'Is that meant to be a joke?' Rowena asked him. 'Have you got no feeling at all?'

Michael's eyes met Charlotte's at last. He said, 'No, not a joke. This isn't a joke. Someone's got here ahead of us, that's all, only he wasn't in any condition to pick daffodils. Where is Peter buried, Charlotte? Have you looked at Peter's grave?'

ABOUT THE AUTHOR

Jan Mark was born in Welwyn, Herts, and grew up in Ashford, Kent, where she attended Canterbury College of Art. She taught in a secondary school in Gravesend for six years, before becoming a freelance writer. She has won the Carnegie Medal twice, the *Observer* Teenage Fiction Award, the Penguin/*Guardian* award, and the Angel Literary Prize twice.

Haunting fiction for older readers from Red Fox

THE XANADU MANUSCRIPT
John Rowe Townsend

There is nothing unusual about visitors in Cambridge.

So what is it about three tall strangers which fills John with a mixture of curiosity and unease? Not only are they strikingly handsome but, for apparently educated people, they are oddly surprised and excited by normal, everyday events. And, as John pursues them, their mystery only seems to deepen.

Set against a background of an old university town, this powerfully compelling story is both utterly fantastic and oddly convincing.

'An author from whom much is expected and received.' *Economist*

ISBN 0 09 9751801 £2.50

ONLOOKER Roger Davenport

Peter has always enjoyed being in Culver Wood, and dismissed the tales of hauntings, witchcraft and superstitions associated with it. But when he starts having extraordinary visions that are somehow connected with the wood, and which become more real to him than his everyday life, he realizes that something is taking control of his mind in an inexplicable and frightening way.

Through his uneasy relationship with Isobel and her father, a Professor of Archaeology interested in excavating Culver Wood, Peter is led to the discovery of the wood's secret and his own terrifying part in it.

ISBN 0 09 9750708 £2.50

Other great reads from ***Red Fox***

THE WINTER VISITOR Joan Lingard

Strangers didn't come to Nick Murray's home town in winter. And they didn't lodge at his house. But Ed Black had—and Nick Murray didn't like it.

Why had Ed come? The small Scottish seaside resort was bleak, cold and grey at that time of year. The answer, Nick begins to suspect, lies with his mother—was there some past connection between her and Ed?

ISBN 0 09 938590 2 £1.99

STRANGERS IN THE HOUSE Joan Lingard

Calum resents his mother remarrying. He doesn't want to move to a flat in Edinburgh with a new father and a thirteen-year-old stepsister. Stella, too, dreads the new marriage. Used to living alone with her father she loathes the idea of sharing their small flat.

Stella's and Calum's struggles to adapt to a new life, while trying to cope with the problems of growing up are related with great poignancy in a book which will be enjoyed by all older readers.

ISBN 0 09 955020 2 £1.95

Enter the gripping world of the REDWALL saga

REDWALL Brian Jacques

It is the start of the summer of the Late Rose. Redwall Abbey, the peaceful home of a community of mice, slumbers in the warmth of a summer afternoon. The mice are preparing for a great jubilee feast.

But not for long. Cluny is coming! The evil one-eyed rat warlord is advancing with his battle-scarred mob. And Cluny wants Redwall . . .

ISBN 0 09 951200 9 £3.50

MOSSFLOWER Brian Jacques

One late autumn evening, Bella of Brockhall snuggled deep in her armchair and told a story . . .

This is the dramatic tale behind the bestselling *Redwall.* It is the gripping account of how Redwall Abbey was founded through the bravery of the legendary mouse Martin and his epic quest for Salmandastron. Once again, the forces of good and evil are at war in a stunning novel that will captivate readers of all ages.

ISBN 0 09 955400 3 £3.50

MATTIMEO Brian Jacques

Slagar the fox is intent on revenge . . .

On bringing death and destruction to the inhabitants of Redwall Abbey, in particular to the fearless warrior mouse Matthias. Gathering his evil band around him, Slagar plots to strike at the heart of the Abbey. His cunning and cowardly plan is to steal the Redwall children—and Mattimeo, Matthias' son, is to be the biggest prize of all.

ISBN 0 09 967540 4 £3.50